Strange School, Secret Wish

Strange School, Secret Wish

Bernice Gold

An imprint of
Beach Holme Publishing
Vancouver

This book is published by Beach Holme Publishing, 226–2040 West 12th Avenue, Vancouver, B.C. V6J 2G2. *www.beachholme.bc.ca*. This is a Sandcastle Book.

The publisher gratefully acknowledges the financial support of the Canada Council for the Arts and of the British Columbia Arts Council. The publisher also acknowledges the financial assistance received from the Government of Canada through the Book Publishing Industry Development Program (BPIDP) for its publishing activities.

The Canada Council | Le Conseil des Arts
for the Arts | du Canada

BRITISH
COLUMBIA
ARTS COUNCIL
Supported by the Province of British Columbia

Editor: Jen Hamilton
Production and Design: Jen Hamilton
Cover Art: Ljuba Levstek
Author Photograph: Allen Gold

Printed and bound in Canada by AGMV Marquis Imprimeur

National Library of Canada Cataloguing in Publication Data

Gold, Bernice.
  Strange school, secret wish

ISBN 0-88878-425-2

I. Title.
PS8563.O523S77 2001   jC813'.54 C2001-911075-8
PZ7.G642St 2001

For Elizabeth Hillman and her family,
who inspired this story

One

March 26, 1927
Little Moose Lake
Ontario, Canada

Dear Pen Pal,

The wolves are howling tonight. They're noisier than usual, so I guess they must be closer.

Jenny put down her pen. "Brian," she called, "do you think he'll believe me?"

"Do I think who will believe what?"

"My pen pal in Toronto. Do you think he'll believe me about the wolves?"

"Well, he might or he might not," her brother said. "I wouldn't if I lived in Toronto."

1

Bernice Gold

"Much help you are." Jenny sucked the end of her pen, dipped it in the inkwell, and started again.

Dear Pen Pal,

I'm not like you. That's because I live on a railway car in Northern Ontario with my family. Half of the car is a school room and the other half is our home. It's really nice. We have a kitchen and a bathroom with a bathtub. It's easy to get water because there are lakes and rivers everywhere. I should know, because I'm the one who gets the water. I have a yoke that goes over my shoulders that a pail fits in on either side. The rest of our home is one big room where we live, eat, and sleep.

I guess this sounds pretty funny to you, but it's true. My father is the schoolteacher. He's really the principal, too, because we have all the grades up to eight in one room.

There aren't any other schools up here because it's all forest and no roads. The people are scattered in little settlements. Mostly they're railway workers and trappers. Some have children, but it's too hard to have a regular school when there's nine children in one place and then after thirty miles maybe seven in the next place. That's why we have the railway-car school. Dad calls it the "school-on-wheels" because—

"Brian?"
"*Now* what!"
"When I write this all down, I mean, about the school car and how we live, it sounds like a story in a book."

2

"Well, it isn't. It's the way things are. If you're supposed to be telling him how we live, why don't you just do it? And stop asking me dumb questions."

"You!" Jenny aimed an eraser at him but missed. Still, Brian was right, she thought. She'd just write how it was. Anyway, what else could she do? She turned back to her letter.

Right now our school car is parked on a siding at Little Moose Lake. There are about forty people here and seven of them are kids. We'll stay here a week so they can come to school, and then the engine will come and move us on to Greenwood. Then, in four weeks, we'll be back here again.

You might think the kids are lucky because they have only one week of school, and four or five without. Well, they don't think so. When we pull in, everybody's so glad to see us it's like a holiday. And they're really sad when we leave. Not just the children —everybody.

I would hate ordinary school. This is more fun. I have everything I want here.

Jenny put down her pen and rested her chin on her hand. Everything? Well, that wasn't exactly true. But it was none of his business, she told herself.

She picked up the pen and wrote.

Well, I have to go now.

Yours sincerely,
Jenny Merrill

She pushed the letter to one side. Everything she wanted? Everything except for... She'd get the big book and look at its picture right now. And read the description—as if she didn't know it by heart.

"Jenny, give me a hand over here."

Jenny jumped. "Coming!"

"If we don't get your father to fix that oven door, I'll have to stop baking," her mother said. "There now, the bread's in. Just close the door gently. Thanks, dear. Now what are you up to?"

"I think I'll have a look at the wishing book."

"All right," her mother said, "but remember that it's more a wishing than a getting book."

"I know," Jenny said as she heaved it off the shelf where it lived beside *The Book of Home Remedies*.

But there was one thing in there she just had to get.

She plunked the book on the table. Its cover said: *The T. Eaton Co. Mail Order Catalogue for 1927. Spring and Summer*.

The wishing book, Jenny thought, for faraway people like her family who couldn't go to the big, fancy Eaton's store in Toronto. Of course, they didn't have any money, extra money, that is. Her father had always said they were rich in all the things that counted. She guessed that was true, but couldn't they be rich in money, too? Not much, just a little bit.

She gazed thoughtfully at the picture on the cover and wondered if Mr. T. Eaton could walk into his store, maybe with his whole family, and take anything they liked.

"John," he'd say to his son, "would you like that train set? Amy, would you like this big doll? And, Jenny dear,

What would you like?"

"Oh, Mr. Eaton, I'd like—" quickly she turned to page 244 in the catalogue and pointed "—that!" she said out loud. "That's my heart's desire."

"What, dear?" Her mother turned away from the stove, hands all floury. "What's your heart's desire?"

"Oh, nothing," Jenny muttered, fire-red, as she got up and whistled the whole thing off.

In bed that night Jenny conjured up her secret treasure. It came right off the page. She felt its curves, its satin finish. She raised her arm and drew the bow across its strings. Her violin. Hers. The finest Eaton's had to offer.

But how in the world could it ever be? Eighteen dollars and fifty cents! How could she find the money? What way did she have of getting it?

And that wasn't all, she told herself. She'd need a lot more money for lessons. Even great musicians took lessons at first. Well, she'd have to find a way, because she was going to be one of them.

Two

The next morning at just after five o'clock there was a long, low whistle down the line. Ten minutes later the school car shook, shuddered, and started to roll.

Jenny opened one eye. Nothing broken that she could see. She closed it again and thought, *Should have put in the letter "big bang when the engine hitches us."* Lulled by the rhythm of the rolling wheels, she soon fell asleep again.

She awoke to the smell of hot cereal, scrambled eggs, and toast. The engine had brought them to Greenwood, and everyone was at breakfast, including Mr. Todd, the engineer.

"Now, Matthew," he was saying to her father, "don't let me forget to drop off your groceries. And the coal. That's mighty important. And, Edith, Mary sent you this recipe. Says you should try it." He put down his coffee cup. "Well, folks, I better be moving. Got to pick up some freight down the line."

"Gee, Mr. Todd," Brian said, sounding aggrieved, "you said you'd help me with my plane model and now there's no time."

"Don't worry, Brian. I'll be back. Probably evening next time I pull you out. Plenty of time then."

"Meg," Mrs. Merrill said to her youngest, "please stop looking out the window and finish your breakfast. You'll see your friends soon enough. Jenny, will you put the dishes in the sink before school starts? Oh, and Brian, you'd better fire up the school stove."

"There's more coal in the vestibule," Jenny's father called out. "March isn't springtime yet here." Mr. Merrill looked out the window as he talked. "There's quite a crowd out there. Always is at Greenwood. You know, Edith," he said to his wife, "this first day in a new place is always exciting. Every single time. It's not just the children. Look out there—friends, relatives, parents, and four, five, seven dogs. Oh, there's Mrs. Twotrees." He waved to a Native woman with a baby on her back. "I have a message for her."

"Dad, look," Brian said, "there's two new kids."

"All right, I'm going. Jenny, ring the school bell in six minutes." Grabbing his jacket, Mr. Merrill hurried down the train steps to greet old friends and the seven regular schoolchildren, and to welcome the new students. As he moved nearer, a chorus of voices rang out.

"Hi, Mr. Merrill."

"Hello there, Matthew."

"Lookit here, Mr. Merrill."

"So good to see you."

"My cat had kittens."

"Brownies, fresh, will you give them to Edith?"

Through the smiling, jostling crowd Mr. Merrill made his way to a bearded man standing apart, a child on either side.

"I'm Matthew Merrill," he said, holding out his hand, "the schoolteacher. Are these my new pupils?"

The father smiled, offered his hand, and spoke his name.

A neighbour, Mr. McNab, helped out. "They're new here. Trappers from Finland. Don't speak English. He came in from Crooked Lake by snowshoe to bring the kids to school, maybe nine miles. They'll stay over with me while the school train's in."

Mr. Merrill took each child by the hand. "Tell him not to worry. We'll look after them and make sure they're comfortable." Then, as Jenny rang the bell, Mr. Merrill said, "All right, school time."

Goodbyes were murmured, parents drifted away, and the children trooped into the school car. The school room stood waiting. A map was unrolled, fresh chalk was at the blackboard, books were on the shelves, and down the middle of the long, narrow rail car sat two rows of desks.

The children all rushed to their usual seats, except for the new ones. Mr. Merrill led them to two desks near the front, side by side.

"This is our school," he said to them. "I'm Mr. Merrill, the teacher, and this is..." Starting from the back of the room where the older pupils sat, each student came forward, spoke his or her name, and shook hands. All except Jenny.

At her seat near the back of the room Jenny was dreaming. She wondered how it felt to be new and not understand what people were saying. But soon her thoughts drifted back to their resting place—the violin on page 244 of the Eaton's catalogue.

Vaguely Jenny heard someone say, "The young lady in the rear left seat!" Then, louder, "The young lady in the rear left seat!"

Goodness, she thought, that must be her father. What could he want? Oh, her name! She jumped up. "Jenny Eaton!" she shouted, then turned red to the roots of her hair.

When the laughter died down, she said, looking straight ahead and speaking very clearly, "Well, I made a mistake. Anybody could."

"Quite true," Mr. Merrill replied. "Quite true. And now, let's get on with things. Grade Ones, get out the new reading books. Grade Twos, start with arithmetic. Now, let's see. We have no Grade Threes. Grade Fours, up here at the map of Canada." And so it went, all the way up to grade eight. Then he sat with the two new children, and together they looked at some picture books.

Jenny and Jim, both in grade seven, were given mental arithmetic problems to solve. The first one began: "If A runs 3 1/7 times as fast as B and C runs 1/3 as fast as—"

Poor C, Jenny mused. She never won. Jenny figured A would win again. Maybe even B. She felt sorry for C but guessed she'd rather be A. Or whichever one would get the violin.

Jim nudged her. "Jen? Finished?" She picked up her pencil and went to work.

Later that afternoon Brian noticed a large, dark shape not far from the school car. "Hey, Mom," he called, "there's a moose out there."

"Not again," she sighed. "It must be after those cabbage

leaves I threw into the woods." She peered out the window. "Well, he's not bothering anybody. I hope he goes away before the people come tonight."

Just before supper Mr. Merrill strolled by the kitchen counter and sneaked a fresh-baked cookie.

"Matthew! Leave those alone. They're for tonight."

"Sorry, Edith, I'm just strengthening myself for bingo. I enjoy a party, but, oh, that game!"

"I know," his wife said. "But what else is there that everyone can play? Even your two new Finnish pupils can join in."

"Absolutely true. Anyway, you know I love these get-togethers."

Meg came by with a gap-toothed smile.

"What's so pleasing?" her father asked.

"Bingo. Me and my gerbils love bingo nights. They like it when I move their cage to where all the people are."

The dishes were hardly dry before the crowd started arriving. Mrs. Twotrees, her husband, the baby, and her sister were among the first. They were followed by Mr. McNab with the two new children who brightened up when they saw Meg and Brian.

Don Roberts, the youngest railway hand, stepped up with his new wife. "I'd like you to meet Janet," he said to the Merrills. "She's just up from the south." He looked at her fondly. "First thing she said was 'Donnie, I never saw so many trees.' But she likes it here."

"Yes, I do," Janet said, "but it's awfully black at night with no lights anywhere. And lonely. The best time is when your train comes in. It's more homelike then."

The Wilsons came in slowly, supporting Mr. Wilson's

elderly mother.

"It's my night out," she told Mr. Merrill. "I'm celebrating."

"It's her ninetieth birthday," her son said proudly.

"Well, let's tell everybody." Mr. Merrill offered his arm. "Mrs. Agnes Wilson," he announced. "Ninety years old today!"

The crowd clapped and cheered. And when Brian hurried back from the kitchen, shielding one candle in a cupcake, they roared, "Happy birthday to you!"

Mr. Wilson glanced at his mother. Her wrinkled face glowed. "Thank you," he said to the crowd. "Thank you very much."

After that, people settled down to the serious business of playing bingo. Meg handed out the cards, Mr. Merrill was the caller, and Brian hovered around the two new students so he could help when needed.

Except for two or three crying babies and some shoving and pushing between best friends Jim and Franco, every-thing went smoothly. Too soon for most, the game was over.

Mrs. Twotrees, the big winner, smiled her thanks when she opened her prize—booties for the new baby. Players relaxed with hot drinks and goodies. Nobody seemed in a hurry to leave.

While Jenny and her mother were working in the kitchen, Mrs. Wilson came in. "Pickles," she said, holding out a jar.

"Now, that's nice," Mrs. Merrill said. "I love a good pickle. Hard to get up here."

"Easy enough to make," Mrs. Wilson said. "When we were near Stratford, we used to grow cucumbers. Then we'd pick them and pickle them. Now, Edith..."

Jenny sighed and wished Mrs. Wilson would leave. She knew it meant a lot to everyone to visit, but why didn't they think of her family? They couldn't go to bed until everyone went home, and it was her special turn to sleep alone.

Sleeping alone. Each of the Merrill children had a turn in the one curtained-off berth. "Privacy," her father had said. "We haven't much of it, but at least one night a week you'll each have a chance to be alone."

Finally goodbyes were said, the last dishes were washed, and the evening was over.

Jenny, in her nightgown, took from her drawer a length of rose-coloured satin. She touched its folds, unrolled its length, and swirled it around her shoulders. Thus arrayed, she walked like a queen to her bedchamber. Once inside with the curtains drawn, she removed her mantle and drew a great sigh of relief.

At last she was alone, she thought. Alone with herself, and nobody knew what she was thinking.

She conjured up the violin, could almost see it, almost feel it. Somewhere in the distance she was certain she heard a melody, soft and low.

Then came the thorny question. How could she ever get it? But even as she mused, the image faded and was replaced by quite another—a jar of pickles. There were words to go with it.

"I love a good pickle."

"Everybody does."

"Up here they're so hard to get."

"Easy enough to make, you just—"

Jenny sat straight up in bed. What if she— It sounded easy. Her family *did* summer down in Glendale. It wasn't rocky the way it was here, and there were farms everywhere. All she'd need would be some land, not even much. She could probably stick the seeds in the ground and the cucumbers would shoot up. Then she'd put them in jars.

When school started again, she could sell them at every place they stopped. How much should she ask for a jar? If she knew, she could figure out how many jars she would have to sell. But then there were her lessons, too. Jenny lay back and closed her eyes. She would think about that tomorrow.

The next day after school, after helping with the ironing, after playing Chinese checkers with Meg, after arguing with Brian about whose turn it was to feed the gerbils, Jenny sat down to write another letter.

March 28, 1927
The T. Eaton Co,
Toronto, Ontario

Dear Mr. Eaton,

I hope you are well. I know there is an order form for your catalogue, but I can't use it because I haven't got the money yet for what I want. What I want is the violin on page 244 of the spring catalogue for 1927. It costs $18.50. I know it's expensive, but it's so beautiful, and I'm sure it has the best sound. It says so in the adver-

tisement.

By the end of the summer, I will have lots of money, so what I am asking is, will you save my violin for me, in case they all get bought? I am thanking you because I'm sure you will, and it does relieve my mind.

Yours sincerely,
Jenny Abigail Merrill

Three

The next mail delivery might be as much as a week away. Could there be a reply by then? Jenny knew she couldn't count on it. Mr. Eaton was probably a very busy man. The time crawled by.

When the mailbag arrived at last, she held her breath, hardly daring to hope. But, yes, there was a crisp white envelope for Miss Jenny A. Merrill.

She took it, snatched up her jacket, and darted outside to the privacy of a big flat rock, hedged by cedars.

Dear Miss Merrill,

Thank you for your inquiry of March 28th concerning the item entitled "Violin Outfit for Advanced Student" as advertised in the 1927 Spring/Summer catalogue.

Unfortunately we are unable to comply with your request to "save," as you put it, the item in question. However, should the purchase of the article become possible in the future, we will be pleased to forward it. Assuming, of course, that this item is still available.

Please be assured that the T. Eaton Co. is always happy to be of service.

Sincerely yours,

D. B. Mann
General Manager
Order Department
T. Eaton Co.

Jenny sat there, chilled and shaking, and read the letter again. Hot tears splashed onto the rock.

Stop it, she told herself. She wanted this to be a secret. Some secret it would be if they saw her blubbering like this. "What's wrong?" they'd say. "What's wrong, Jenny?" She sniffed, gulped, and went in to help with supper.

If her eyes did tear as she chopped the supper onions, well, chopping onions made most eyes run. But her knife flashed so high and so wide that her mother cried, "Jenny, look out!"

Later that evening her father said, "The stars are lovely tonight. Anyone care to join me for a look? How about you, Jenny?"

She shook her head.

"Oh, come on. Just a little stretch."

Slowly she put on her boots and jacket, and they stepped out into the blackness.

Although the calendar said April, it was winter underfoot, and the lamps from within shed pools of light on the snow. They walked along in the blackness beside the railway track. Mr. Merrill looked up at the starry sky. "Wonderful night."

"Not for me," Jenny said.

"Is there something I could help with?"

Jenny sniffed. "No."

"Rather I didn't ask?"

"Yes, I'd rather. It's my business." They turned back toward the car, both faces set.

As April waxed, thoughts of music waned, and Jenny herself grew silent.

Others noticed. "What's the matter with Jenny?" Meg asked Brian one evening. "She won't play with the gerbils, and she says she hates Chinese checkers."

"I don't know," he said. "Maybe she just doesn't feel like talking right now. Better leave her alone."

Jenny, quite unseen, was walking outside the car and overheard the conversation. Their words shocked her.

Why were they so upset? she asked herself. She was the one who had troubles.

As she mused, her feet found the path toward the tiny cluster of houses on the rise. The light from their oil lamps spilled into the darkness. They were all warm and happy in there, Jenny thought, but she wasn't.

As she came closer, the door of the nearest house opened and a voice called, "Jenny Merrill, you come right in here out of the cold. I saw you coming. The cocoa's on, and there's fresh-baked cookies. There now." Mrs. Beeson handed her a steaming cup.

"Smells good," Jenny said. She raised the cup to her lips and burst into tears.

"Well, then, well, then," Mrs. Beeson burbled. She rescued the cup, offered a handkerchief, and sat down to hear the whole violin story. Filled with "if onlys" and "how can I's," it poured right out. Mrs. Beeson looked startled, but only for a moment. Then she leaned forward and listened, plump with sympathy.

At the end of the torrent of words Jenny sighed hugely. "Could I have the cocoa back now?" She gulped it down and got to her feet. "Gosh, it must be late. Thanks a lot for the cocoa, Mrs. Beeson." At the door she paused. "You won't tell anyone, will you? I mean, it's a secret."

"My lands," Mrs. Beeson said, "a secret's a secret, and that's how it's going to stay."

Light with relief, Jenny hummed to herself as she crunched her way home in the darkness.

She must have climbed the steps very quietly because when she came in no one even looked up. Her family was grouped around the big Coleman lamp that gently hissed and glowed: Meg with her crayons, Brian with a plane model, her mother with knitting, and her father with schoolwork.

A feeling rose in Jenny that came right up into her throat. How much she loved them! Why was it so hard to let them know? "Hello everyone," she said. "Meggie, want to play Chinese checkers before you go to bed?"

That night, in bed, a little rising tune entwined her

thoughts. She knew she could get the money. All she needed to know was how to grow the cucumbers and make them into pickles. Before her eyes a shining row of pickle jars marched along an endless shelf.

She yawned. People liked pickles. Everyone said so. Then a new thought stabbed her. But making pickles—could she keep it a secret? There must be a way. She sighed, punched her pillow, and drifted off.

By mid-April the tree buds were beginning to swell with the first signs of spring. Jenny saw them and burned with impatience. Spring almost, and then summer, the growing season. And what did she know about growing?

There were things to find out and things to be done—and quickly.

But that in itself was a problem. Once she started asking questions it wouldn't be her own. Everyone would know. But she had to talk about it, or she'd burst.

The next morning at three minutes before bell time, Jenny still sat at the table, her breakfast uneaten. Two minutes before bell time Mr. Merrill picked up his papers and started for the school room. A half minute later Jenny raced after him, grabbed his sleeve, and burst out, "Dad, how do you grow cucumbers?"

He stared at her. "Jenny, what in the world? Is it something special? There goes the bell. Suppose we talk tonight. Is it going to be just you and me, or is it going to be all of us?"

As the first kids rushed into the school room, Jenny blew her nose and said, "It might as well be all of us."

That evening after supper and before the dishes were done, Jenny told the whole story. How, at a concert down in Toronto she'd fallen in love with the violin and had made up her mind that she would be a violinist. A great violinist, playing onstage all by herself.

"Couldn't anyone play with you?" Brian asked.

"Maybe," Jenny said. "Sometimes. I had to really think about it," she went on. "So I decided to see if there were violins in the Eaton's catalogue, and there, right on page 244, were three different ones."

"How could you play three at the same time?" Meg asked.

"Meg, you're so silly. Anyway, I read what it said about them, and I chose the very best, the deep-toned Stradivarius-type model." Jenny sighed. "Because it's for advanced or professional players."

"But how can you be an advanced player when you haven't even begun?" Brian asked.

"Because I expect to learn fast, and then soon I'll be a professional."

"But where will you get the money?"

"That's the part I was coming to. You see, I wrote to Mr. Eaton and told him which one I wanted. I explained I didn't have the money yet but asked if he'd put one aside in case they were all gone. Then I'd pay him when I had the money.

"But he wrote back—well, another man signed the letter—but I know Mr. Eaton really wrote it. He said it wasn't possible to save one and, well..." Jenny's voice trembled. "He just didn't seem to care."

Her father sat, chin in hand. Her mother sipped her coffee.

Brian broke the silence. "How much does this thing cost?"

"It costs a lot. With the bow and the case and everything, it's eighteen dollars and fifty cents."

Brian whistled. Her father's eyebrows shot up, and her mother's coffee cup came down.

"Well, dear," her mother said, "if you asked the Eaton's man to hold one for you, you must have some idea about raising the money."

Jenny nodded. "I have. I told it to Dad."

"Me?" He looked surprised. "You didn't tell me anything."

"Yes, I did. This morning."

"Aha, cucumbers."

Jenny turned to her mother. "It's because of your friend, Mom, who talked about the pickles."

"What pickles?"

"The ones Mrs. Wilson gave you. She said it was as easy growing cucumbers as falling off a log." Jenny's voice quickened. "So that's what I'm going to do. I'll grow the cucumbers, and then I'll pickle them and sell the jars of pickles."

Everybody spoke at once.

"Where are you going to grow cucumbers?"

"When could you do it?"

"Who's going to buy them?"

Then there was a last thought from Brian. "But, Jen, how could you do all that? I mean, you don't even know anything about—"

Jenny's temper flared. "I can do it! I'll find out how." But then she sagged a little and played with a spoon.

"Is there a problem?" her father asked.

"No, well...no. It's just that I...I kind of wanted this to be my secret."

"Then why are you telling us?" her mother asked.

Jenny looked sheepish. "Well...I might need some help."

The Merrills sat in silence for a moment.

"My gerbils will help," Meg murmured. "They'll eat all the cucumbers."

Everyone laughed. Then Jenny's mother got to her feet. "Bedtime," she said, "and well after." She started to pull out the folding beds.

Her father walked up and down the narrow aisle. "This takes thinking about, Jenny. Yes, it does."

"Matthew, dear, you're in the way," his wife told him. "Give over now. Brian, will you stoke the furnace one last time? Jenny, turn down the lamps." She put an arm around her shoulder. "Come on now, dear, there's still tomorrow." And soon the room was in darkness.

But although the Merrills were all in bed, at least one couldn't sleep. Restless, Jenny tossed and turned. Her mind replayed her parents' words, and even more, their silences.

They had hardly said anything. Why? she asked herself Had she done something wrong? Was it wrong to want the violin? Maybe the pickles were wrong. Perhaps she should give up the whole idea.

As she lay there brooding, an impish little tune floated up in the dark. Once again she saw the catalogue, the picture, and the words: *A Stradivarius model...splendid tone...in a rich brown shade*.

She had to have it. And it would have to be soon. She needed to start her training young or she wouldn't be any good. Everybody knew that. And if nobody wanted to help her, she didn't care. She'd do it herself. Jenny yanked up the blankets and closed her eyes.

🎻 /

At ten minutes to three the next afternoon Mr. Merrill glanced at his watch. "All right, everyone, school's over for today."

Franco Minelli's hand shot up and waved like a tree in a storm. "Hey, Mr. Merrill, what about a volleyball game in the snow, and you be the coach?"

"Oh, I suppose—"

"Great! I'll ask Mrs. Merrill if we can borrow her clothes-line and the poles. Come on, everybody, outside!" Nine of the ten children rushed for jackets, toques, mittens, and boots, then clattered down the steps and into the wan April sunshine.

Only the tenth remained at her desk—Jenny. A snow-ball hit the window, and Franco called, "Jenny, come on." But she shook her head.

After a while the sun melted her gloom enough to move her outside, where she sat shivering on a rock, her nose in a book.

A stray ball landed near her feet, and her father came running up to retrieve it. "Hi, Jen," he panted. "Good book?"

"I don't think you'd be interested."

"I'm always interested."

"How can you say such a thing?" Jenny blazed out. "When I tried to tell you about the violin and the pickles, you didn't seem interested then."

A chorus of three voices chanted, "Mr. Merrill, could we please have the ball?"

"What? Oh, yes, yes, the ball. Sorry." He threw it to the

waiting hands. "You're quite mistaken. Of course, we're interested. If you want to be a violinist, that's fine. And you're quite right about raising the money yourself. Schoolteachers aren't rich, especially this one. And even if I were, I'd want you to find out for yourself if—" He broke off, then continued. "It's not the violin or your pickle project."

Jenny's voice rose to a squeak. "Well, then, what is it? What made you so mean?"

"Mean? I don't think so. You put us on the spot. You have a project, and you'd like to do it all by yourself. But you feel you can't, so you ask us for help. You ask for our help, Jenny, but you don't want it. There's the rub."

On the field there was shouting and shoving. Somebody called, "Mr. Merrill, we need you."

"Coming, I'm coming." He hurried off.

Jenny kicked at the slushy snow. There was a lot to think about, but she didn't know where to start. Another ball landed near her feet. Slowly she picked it up and lobbed it back.

Four

There was quite a stir back in the train car because the engine, the one that would pull them to Lost River, was on its way.

"I hope Mr. Todd's the engineer," Meg said.

"I hope the others finish that game soon," her mother said with a worried frown. "We thought we had three or four hours yet. Oh, Jenny, there you are. The engine's coming any minute. Call your father and Brian, will you? They don't know we're on the move. I hope the hitching is easy this time. I've got a cake in the oven."

But when the engine did come, it came with a crash. Mrs. Merrill sighed. "There goes my cake, and who knows what else?"

"*I* know," Meg said, getting out the broom and dustpan. "Three glasses, two plates, and one record. I hope it wasn't 'When the Red, Red Robin Comes Bob Bob Bobbing Along.'" She picked up the broken record. "Goody! It wasn't."

"I'm glad," her mother said. "But, oh, Jenny, look at my plants all over the floor!"

"Never mind," Jenny said. "I'll fix everything up."

There was a knock on the door, and the engineer came in. It wasn't Mr. Todd this time.

"Shook you up, did I? Sorry about that, Mrs. Merrill. These freight engines are sometimes a bit rough."

"Can't be helped," she replied. "We know you do your best to ease us in. Look at it this way, where would we be without you? Oh, good, here come Matthew and Brian, so let's all sit down and have a piece of fallen cake."

When they finished, the engineer thanked her and said, "Now, is everyone aboard? Because we're ready to roll." And soon after he left, the huge black engine started gently as a breeze.

Half an hour later, as the train slowed for their next stop, Meg yelled, "There's the Leaning Tree! I love coming into Lost River."

"Johnnie! Hey, Johnnie!"

"Brian, don't shout," Mrs. Merrill said. "We'll be there in a minute, and he can't hear you, anyway."

"Well, I have to see him. I lent him my hockey stick, and I want it back now."

"Matthew, there's Denise McCall. She's making a quilt for your birthday."

"Do I want a quilt?"

"You'd love to have a quilt."

The minute the train stopped, people climbed aboard. First in was a burly man with a large casserole dish that he carefully placed on the table.

"John Kusiak!" Mr. Merrill shook his hand. "I didn't

know you were back."

"Came back yesterday. Slept two nights in the bush. Checked all my traplines—not a bad haul for this time of year. Glad to be back, though. I heard the whistle down the line and came right over. Eddie's here, too. Can't wait for school tomorrow." He turned to Mrs. Merrill. "The wife sent this over. She said to just pop it in the oven. It'll save you making supper."

"Oh, boy." Brian rubbed his stomach. "It smells good."

"Well, I'm on my way. Matthew, can we sneak in a few games of chess?"

"I can hardly wait."

As Mr. Kusiak left, a young trapper's wife came in. She touched Jenny's arm. "Bingo tonight?"

"No, not tonight."

"Has Mr. Merrill got any of those moving pictures? I just love them."

"Well, he might, but they'd be for later on in the week. I think tonight's the special night for grown-ups who want help learning English. It must be hard when you come from another country and you can't understand what's going on."

"Do they read the kids' books?"

"Not really. People bring in letters and papers they don't understand, and my parents help to work them out. Then there's the Eaton's catalogue. My dad says it's the best learning book."

"And with pictures, too." The young wife smiled. "It would be more fun learning that way."

"I think so, too."

"Well, goodbye, Jenny. I hope bingo night is soon."

Later, when everyone was gone, Mr. Merrill said to his wife, "You must admit, Edith, that living like this warms the heart."

"It does," she said, "even when it breaks the dishes."

School on Monday morning brought Eddie Kusiak, the three Morin kids, Johnnie Highwater, and Janie Wilson. Old-timers, all of them, they were at the steps long before the bell rang.

"Easy now," Mr. Merrill said. "Anyone would think this was a holiday, not a school day."

"It's the same thing," Eddie said, "when you have to wait four weeks for the school car to come."

"Look," Francine Morin said, tapping Mr. Merrill's arm, "I got on all clean clothes. My mother, she ironed them before breakfast. My hair, too."

"She ironed your hair?"

"Oh, you're just making jokes, Mr. Merrill. She washed it."

"Well, you certainly look nice and fresh, Francine."

"Mr. Merrill!" Janie held up a bunch of exercise books. "I done all my—I did all my homework like you said."

"Mr. Merrill," Johnnie Highwater asked, "where's Vic?"

"Oh, he'll be here any minute, I suppose. The bell hasn't gone yet."

"But he told me he'd come especially early to show me something."

"Maybe he started off late."

"Maybe, but it blew hard all night. He has to come seven miles across the lake, and my father said his pine-branch markers might have blown away. Then the frozen lake looks all the same. And his lead dog is sick."

Mr. Merrill looked anxious. "Now, that's something to

worry about. Johnnie, if Vic isn't here by the bell, we'll send out a search party." He glanced at his watch. "Four minutes."

The door was flung open, and Vic walked in. "Hi, Johnnie, sorry I'm late. What's the matter? Everybody looks worried." He sounded jaunty, but he didn't look it.

"We were worried about you," Mr. Merrill said.

"Me and my dog team? We do this all the time."

"But we thought the markers might have blown away," Johnnie explained.

"Most of then did," Vic admitted. He slumped against the door. "Mr. Merrill, is it okay that I tied my dogs up near the shed today? They're kind of tired." He shivered and coughed.

Mr. Merrill felt his shirt. "Vic, you're wet right through. Brian, will you get a dry shirt for Vic? Now, you come and sit by the stove for a while. Mrs. Merrill's going to bring you a hot drink. And another thing, Vic, spring's nearly here. Your next trip will be by canoe."

Not five minutes later, Brian said, "Dad, there's someone waiting outside."

"Where? Oh, yes, I see. All right, everyone, I'll be right back." He hurried down the steps.

A thin, dark boy stood near the school car, holding a pair of skis.

Mr. Merrill held out his hand. "You must be new in the area. Welcome. I'm Matthew Merrill, the teacher, and this is our school on wheels. Will you come in?"

"I dunno if I can," the boy said.

"Why can't you?"

"My friend, he went to your school. He told me that

every morning you raise the flag and you sing 'God Save the King.'"

"Yes, we do. Is that a problem?"

"Yeah."

"Why would that be?"

"Because my other teacher from when I was down south in Sudbury, she says to me, 'Tony, you got a voice like a crow, and besides that, you've got no tune in it. When we have the concert and the other kids sing, you don't sing. You understand, Tony? Just stand there. Don't sing.' When my father hears I can't sing in the concert, he gets mad at me. He says, 'What's the matter with you? You're Italian and you can't sing?' So how can I come to school if I can't sing 'God Save the King'?" He shifted from one foot to the other and bit an already ragged finger.

"Look," Mr. Merrill said, "it's cold out here. Why don't we go inside? We'll just talk. You don't have to stay."

They climbed up the stairs and went into the warm school car. Mr. Merrill said to the curious class, "This is Tony."

"Tony Corelli," the boy added.

"Right now," Mr. Merrill said, "he's just visiting. Tony, slide into that seat back there while I get things started."

"Grade Ones, you'll begin with your readers. Grade Threes, your arithmetic paper. Grade Fours..."

Once the lessons were assigned, he asked Jenny to take over for five minutes, then shepherded Tony through the school room and into the Merrills' private quarters. "Well, now, Tony, tell me something about yourself."

"Me and my father, we live out at Lake Lucy. I skied in. I don't know what else. Um, my father's a trapper. Anyways, he's trying to be. It's not so easy when you come from the south."

"How far is Lake Lucy?"

Tony shrugged. "Maybe eight, ten miles."

"If you came that far, surely there's something at school that you want?"

"Yeah, I want to learn to sing."

"Anything else?"

"I don't know. I didn't like nothing at the school down south. Anyways, they threw me out."

"I see. Well, suppose we start with singing? My daughter, Jenny, is very musical. She might be willing to help. Now, I've got to go back to the school room. Will you come?"

"I guess."

Jenny, when asked about the singing lessons, was surprised but not unpleased. It was arranged that for one week Tony would have lunch with the Merrills, and right after Jenny would give him a singing lesson.

"But you understand," Mr. Merrill said, "this means attending school before and after lunch."

"What am I supposed to do at school?" Tony asked.

"We'll find out what you can do," Mr. Merrill said.

That evening at supper Jenny asked, "Do you think he'll show up tomorrow, Dad?"

Her father answered, just as easily as if there had been no coolness between them. "I think he will."

Tony did come—that day and every day after. Mr. Merrill tried to start him on a large primer, but Tony said, "No thanks. I don't read no baby books."

"Well, then, try this," Mr. Merrill said, handing him a copy of *Treasure Island*.

Tony sat at the back of the room, poring over the book and muttering to himself. When Jenny asked him how he was getting on, he said, "There's too many crazy words. Who knows what they mean?" So she showed him how to look up the words in the dictionary. The idea intrigued him, and he plugged away, dictionary at hand.

When Mr. Merrill asked him about *Treasure Island*, Tony said, "You know something? It's a good story. That boy in the book, he's a lone boy just like me. Say, Mr. Merrill, the guy who wrote the book, how did he know to make him just like me?"

To *Treasure Island* had been added arithmetic. Mr. Merrill had heard Tony tell Francine Morin who was counting on her fat little fingers, "Look, kid, you don't have to do that. There's a better way. I'll show you."

When lunchtime came, Tony followed Jenny into the Merrills' quarters.

Mrs. Merrill greeted him from the stove. "Hello, Tony, nice to have you with us." She motioned to the table. "Everything's ready. Sit right there."

The boy inspected the table carefully. "This I would eat," he said, pointing. "This I wouldn't eat. This, maybe."

"This you would try," Mr. Merrill said, "and this, and this."

Tony shrugged. "Okay, if I got to." He tried a cautious mouthful. "This is good stuff." And he cleaned the plate.

As soon as lunch was over, Tony turned to Jenny. "Can we start?"

They sat at the battered old harmonium. Jenny tapped out the notes as she sang "God Save the King" over and over. "Now you try. It's easy. Just sing with me."

Tony tried hard, but his voice kept slipping. Brian put on

earmuffs. Meg put her head under a pillow.

On Thursday Mrs. Merrill asked Tony how things were going.

"Gee, Mrs. Merrill," he said, "I think I'm getting some tune in my voice...maybe."

After school Mr. Merrill said to him, "Well, Tony, we need a decision from you. Jenny says she'll give you a singing lesson once a week if you stay, and I say school every day if you stay. So what's it going to be?"

Tony drew a deep breath. "I've got to ask you something."

"Yes?"

"Tomorrow, when you raise the flag, could I sing 'God Save the King' with the other kids?" His face darkened. "I don't want no one to laugh at me."

"I can promise no one will laugh at you."

"Okay then. But there's one more thing. After I sing it, I want Jenny to tell me if I sang it right."

The next morning Mr. Merrill, Mrs. Merrill, and the eleven schoolchildren gathered around the flagstaff at the end of the train car for the daily raising of Canada's flag, the Union Jack.

For the occasion Tony wore a fresh shirt. Jenny wore an anxious face. Even Mr. Merrill looked solemn. Teacher and pupils stood side by side as the flag was hoisted up the pole.

Then every voice was raised. Every voice but Jenny's. How could she sing when she needed to listen hard for one special voice? She strained, but there was nothing different. All the voices, including Tony's, were singing the same tune. The right tune.

When the singing ended, Jenny sighed with relief and

smiled at Tony. Quickly she turned away. There were tears in his eyes. He wouldn't want her to see. But she dawdled her way to the steps so he'd have time to catch up with her.

As Tony came up behind her, he nervously cleared his throat. "So, Jenny, what do you think? Did I sing good?"

"You sang perfectly, Tony."

Coming along behind them was Mr. Merrill. "Nice to hear your voice, Tony. Now tell me, do you think you'll be joining our school?"

Tony stopped and considered the question. He kicked a piece of ice from the bottom step. "I guess I could come."

For Jenny the whole day had a kind of glow. And it would even have a special ending, because tonight would be her turn for the private berth.

At bedtime she glided barefoot from the bathroom to the berth. Like a queen to her boudoir, she thought, or a princess, anyway. She closed the sliding curtains and lay back in royal contentment. But not for long. Now that Tony had safely sung, her mind swung back to her own concern—the violin. Wanting it. Telling her plan, her wonderful plan, to the others. The letdown when they hadn't even seemed to care. What was the matter with them? Would she ever feel the same about them? Maybe not.

She shifted uneasily in the bed. Her father's words floated into her mind. *You need our help, but you don't really want it.*

Well, that wasn't true, she told herself. Of course, she wanted their help, because she needed it.

No, that was wrong, too. She hadn't meant it that way.

But another voice dared to answer: *Yes, you did. You don't want anyone's help. You want to keep it a secret and you can't. That's why you're mad.*

Jenny sighed. She guessed that was true. Because it was her idea, she wanted to keep it hers, hers, hers.

And take all the credit, the other voice insisted.

"Oh, shut up, you," Jenny said out loud. "Just shut up."

She sat up in bed. What was the use, anyway? She didn't have anywhere to grow cucumbers. And besides, she didn't know how. And what about the pickling?

She flopped back down on the bed. All she had was an idea and nothing else. Forget it, she told herself. Just forget it. But it wouldn't stay forgotten and the debate raged on. Would it be so bad to accept help? Maybe not, but it would just make everything different.

Again she heard her father's voice saying, "All right, Tony, we'll start with the singing." What if he had said, "Oh, so you've been expelled?" or "Oh, you're not interested in learning?"

What if she had said, "Oh, Dad, I don't want to teach him singing." Would Tony have gone away? Probably, she told herself.

For days her thoughts weighed heavily. No phantom bow touched phantom strings. No pickle jars lined phantom shelves. Life for Jenny was flat and stale.

But not for everyone. Word had gotten around that Mr. Merrill had a real film with Charlie Chaplin in it, just like they showed at the movie theatres down in Toronto. So Saturday night would be something special.

Was that why Saturday brought even more visitors than usual? From breakfast time onward the school-car steps were warmed by a steady stream of feet. Some callers were for Mrs. Merrill—bringing a pie, needing advice, or just wanting to chat. Some were for Mr. Merrill, who held court in the school room: students needing help, worried parents wanting to talk, or a grieving family needing comfort. Others were for the Merrill children—Eddie Kusiak and Janie Wilson, for instance—standing on the bottom step and holding up their skates.

"Hey, Merrills!" Eddie shouted. "The pond's still frozen. Let's go."

"Can't," Brian answered. "We're supposed to be helping. For tonight."

"Oh, go on, you three," their mother put in. "You can help later. Besides, by the next time we're back here, it'll be fishing, not skating."

They all rushed out, even Jenny. "Wait a minute," she called. She went back inside and came out lugging the Victrola with its great big horn.

Janie shouted to the others, "Music, everybody. We're skating to music!"

"This should be fun," Brian said. "We've got these new records from Toronto. My cousin says they're the latest."

He put the Victrola on a flat rock and wound it up. A high-pitched voice started to sing, "Yes, we have no bananas. We have no bananas today." It certainly brought out a great crowd.

On the pond near the school car they swooped and circled, shrieked and slid, to "Yes, We Have No Bananas." Nobody would listen to anything else.

Five

"**E**dith, where are you? It's Jean Beeson. Hello there, Jenny and Meg. Oh, there you are, Edith. I came up on the 3:45. Frank and I are going down to Glendale tomorrow. I just had to see you people before I go."

Jenny, rolling out dough for the evening's goodies, listened carefully. Glendale was the village where the Merrills had their summer cottage.

"You know, my brother has a farm down that way," Mrs. Beeson was saying. "Thought we'd make a trip down. It'll soon be planting season, and then they'll have no time for us."

A farm down that way, Jenny repeated to herself. Planting season...

"Jenny, watch that dough," her mother said. "Not too heavy with the rolling pin."

Should she ask Mrs. Beeson? Jenny wondered. By the time Mrs. Beeson said her goodbyes, she'd made up her mind. The minute the woman stepped outside, Jenny dropped the rolling pin and rushed after her. "Mrs. Beeson," she panted, "remember when I told you about the violin?"

"How could I forget?"

"Well, I have an idea about getting the money to pay for it. I...I want to grow cucumbers and make pickles and sell them. No, please don't smile, Mrs. Beeson. This is serious.

"You see, I was listening when you were talking about your brother's farm, and I was thinking..." Jenny paused for breath. "Maybe he could let me have a little piece of land to grow the cucumbers? I could help look after his children to pay for it."

"Well, now," Mrs. Beeson spoke slowly, "my brother's two sons are taller than he is, so I don't know."

"Oh, please, Mrs. Beeson, there must be something I could do for him."

"He does keep a vegetable stand in the summer. Maybe you could help look after it. Of course, that's if he hasn't got anyone else yet. I can't promise anything, you know, but I'm willing to ask him. That's all I can do. How much land would you need?"

"Enough to grow enough cucumbers to sell enough jars of pickles to pay for my violin and my lessons."

"Well, that's certainly telling me!"

Jenny caught her arm. "Oh, Mrs. Beeson, it would be my heart's delight."

"Your heart's delight, would it?" Mrs. Beeson chuckled, "You sound like a regular theatre play. Well, then, I'll speak to my brother. That's all I can do."

For the rest of the week Jenny walked on air. Cheerfully

she swept the school room, mashed potatoes, delivered soup to old Mrs. Hawkwood, and hauled in constant pails of water for the kitchen and the bathroom.

For Tony, she cheerfully played songs again and again until he could sing them in tune.

In the school room she was filled with goodwill toward all. When Eddie, sitting behind her, dipped her pigtail in the inkwell, she merely smiled and asked him to please stop.

He did but was heard to mutter, "You don't even get mad. You're no fun anymore."

It was while Jenny was playing Pick Up Sticks with Meg that a great idea came to her.

Of course! she thought. She'd write to Mr. Eaton right away and tell him she was sure to get the money now. Meg called out, "Oh-oh, Jenny, you touched one. It's my turn."

Later Jenny settled herself in a corner and started her letter. She began with "Dear Mr. Eaton"— still convinced that although Mr. Mann might have signed the letter, it must be Mr. Eaton who had really written it.

Then she remembered she'd forgotten the date. She put it at the top right: May 2, 1927. And at exactly that moment she came down to earth with a bump.

The second of May? That meant springtime in Glendale, and that was real trouble. Didn't farmers down south start planting about now? How could she hope to get the cucumbers started? Even supposing the farmer let her use the land, it would be too late.

She was so dumb. She would still be in school at planting time. How could she ever plant anything? Nothing was working. Maybe it just hadn't been meant for her to play the violin. Maybe that was her fate.

Jenny spent the rest of the day in a frozen calm. Toward evening she heard her mother say, "Jenny, give us a hand, dear. The engine's coming to move us on."

She did as she was asked and didn't even mind. She felt she was past minding anything.

When the engine arrived and Mr. Todd came in for his usual visit, Jenny could hardly raise her voice to say hello.

He studied her. "Now, Jenny, not taking sick, are you? With spring coming and all?"

She barely raised her head. "Who cares? Who cares about spring?"

"Bad as that, is it? Well, I've something that might change your mind. A package from a Mr. MacAllister from down Glendale way."

Jenny stared at him.

"Instructions inside, it says." He put the bulky package on the table. "There you are."

Meg and Brian both shouted, "Open it, open it!"

Everyone watched as Jenny walked slowly to the table.

"Here." Brian put the scissors in her hand.

When she slit the wrapping, little packets fell out. She picked them up and read the labels: *Cucumber Seeds (for Pickling). J. A. MacAllister.* Underneath was a burlapped package of soil mix, and attached was a letter that Jenny opened and read to herself.

Dear Miss Merrill,

I got your message from my sister, Mrs. Jean Beeson. Seems I could use you to tend my vegetable stand. In return I could let you use a piece of land right by the fence. Good spot for cucumbers.

Guess you'll be down with your folks in July like always. That's a problem. Cucumbers can't wait until then. You're best to start them right now indoors. You just get a bunch of those little cups, fill them with the soil, and put the seeds right in. See they get a lot of light, once they're up. The rest of the instructions are with the package.

Trusting you will find everything in order, I am, yours truly,

James A. MacAllister

P.S. Don't forget to bring the cucumbers along when you come.

The others stood by, waiting. Slowly Jenny picked up a packet and gently shook it.

"Hey, Jenny," Brian burst out, "wake up! What's all this about?"

"They're seeds for starting the cucumbers now."

"How about the whole story?" her father asked.

So Jenny told them about asking Mrs. Beeson to ask her brother for the use of some land to grow cucumbers. "In the afternoons I'll take care of his vegetable stand. It's an exchange."

Her father considered this. "Yes," he said slowly, "that seems to be a fair arrangement."

Mr. Todd picked up a packet and shook it. "There's springtime in there. I brought it early, Jenny." He gulped the last of his coffee. "Get ready, folks. Blueberry Hill here we come."

Later Jenny thought: It really was peculiar. You wanted something and then when you got it, it was a shock. Anyway, how could she have known that Mr. MacAllister would send her the seeds and everything?

She was relieved to find the next day so busy that there was no time for further discussion. Privately she wondered how she could ever follow Mr. MacAllister's instructions.

The subject came up at the supper table. Brian asked, "What are you supposed to do next, Jen?"

"That's the trouble. I'm supposed to get lots of those little cups you can buy, put soil and seeds in each one, and then put them in a sunny place. Indoors, because it's still cold up here. But Mr. MacAllister didn't realize that we hardly have one extra inch of space."

"Oh, I don't know about that," her mother said. "There's the windowsills."

"Oh, Mom, your geraniums are there. I couldn't do that."

"Why not? I could leave my plants right here with Vic Eckonen's Aunt Anna. She'd look after them for me."

"I could make extra shelves to fit on the windows," Brian offered. "That way they'd get lots of light."

"And you and me could plant the seeds," Meg added. "Then we'd water, water, water them."

A wave of gratitude swept over Jenny. Her family was so nice. She wasn't so sure she...but the thought trailed off, unfinished.

It was the most amazing thing! By the end of the week the geraniums had been moved, the shelves put up, the seeds planted, and the windows were lined with rows of little cups. Jenny walked beside the windows, trailing her hand along the sills. It had happened so fast, she thought. It was almost as if they had always been there.

Although it was May, nights could still be frosty. More than once Jenny heard her father moving around at night. If she opened one eye, she could see him shining his flashlight, checking the pipes that heated the train car, making sure the water didn't freeze.

Was he inspecting them more often than usual? So that the plants didn't freeze? Jenny couldn't be sure.

She was grateful for all the help her family was giving. But, at the same time, the thought of it still prickled.

Every day she inspected the plants and wished she could hurry them along. A month seemed so long to wait. But then another thought struck her—in a month school would be over and everything would be so different.

Suddenly a month shrank to hardly any time at all, and now seemed the very best of times. Now there would be an end-of-school party at every stop. Now spring was bursting out all over. Now, along the rail route, willows waved their greening branches and trilliums peered out from the forest floor.

When Billy James came to school on Tuesday, he opened his shirt and said, "Lookit, Mr. Merrill, no more goose grease. I had a bath all over. My mother said you don't need goose grease in the summer."

"How does it feel?"

Billy grinned. "It feels real good."

Sunny days brought out skipping ropes, balls, and Mrs. Merrill's washing. On Friday, the very second school was over, Billy rushed up to the teacher's desk. "Mr. Merrill, Mr. Merrill!"

"Yes, what is it?"

"How about we all go fishing?"

"Oh, I don't know, Billy. It's kind of early for fishing. The ice is hardly out of the water."

"But the fish are there. I saw them."

"Well, it certainly is a lovely day."

"So, can we go?"

"All right, we can go."

"He says yes!" Billy shouted to the others, as if they hadn't heard. "Get ready, everybody."

"Okay, fishermen, I'll meet you outside in five minutes," Mr. Merrill added.

He walked through the car calling, "Edith, where—oh, there you are. The weather's too good to waste. We're all going fishing. The whole school. Want to come? No? See you later."

In high spirits they trooped down to the river, where it gurgled over round stones into a pool below. Sticks were cut, hooks were fastened, and worms were found. Then each fisherman settled into the exact spot where the fish were sure to bite. Lines were cast in silence so as not to frighten the fish.

Almost right away Billy whispered, "I got a bite." He hauled in a good-size fish.

"Lucky! I want one like that," Brian said.

"I want five," Jenny called.

"Shhh, everybody," Mr. Merrill mouthed.

They sat intently for several minutes. Then Mr. Merrill whispered, "I've got a bite. I think it's a big one." He stood and pulled hard.

"Must be a giant," someone said.

Mr. Merrill pulled and pulled, the sweat trickling down his forehead. But nothing happened. He took a step forward and—

"Look out!" Billy yelled.

Too late! Mr. Merrill was in the pool.

He splashed to the shore, and everyone crowded around as he came up dripping and shaking. He laughed. "Must have been a whale. It took my rod."

"Tell that one to Mrs. Merrill," Billy said, and the woods rang with laughter as they escorted him home.

Six

The end of school was on everyone's mind. At supper one evening Brian asked, "Dad, don't you get tired of end-of-school concerts? I mean, at every stop?"

"Mmm, do I? No, I don't think so. It's different every time. Besides, it means a lot to people and to me, too. When I sit there and listen to the songs or the poems, I have to admit I feel very proud. Proud of all of you and our school record, too. After all, except for you three, our students only go to school one week in five or so. Now, that's the end of my speech."

Closing-party fever swept the entire Merrill family. Jenny got so involved in preparations that the sound of the violin almost faded away. Each of the Merrill children took a special part in one of the final concerts. Jenny had asked that the very last one be hers.

"Why the last one?" Meg questioned.

"Because it's at Lost River and I guess my best friends

are there—Vic and Janie."

"And Eddie Kusiak," Brian said. "And Tony Corelli. Don't forget Tony."

"I didn't forget him," Jenny said.

🎻/

"Matthew," Mr. Merrill's wife asked as the car trundled along, "can you believe we're coming into Lost River for the last time before vacation?"

"Second week in June, Edith. It creeps up on you."

"Watch!" Brian called to the other two. "We're coming to the Leaning Tree. Last one to say *tree* is a dummy. Now, now, now, now—"

"Tree!" they shouted in unison.

Right away on Monday morning there was an end-of-school feeling. During the week, lessons grew shorter and concert plans longer. At home dresses, new from the Eaton's catalogue, or shirts, freshly starched, hung stiffly in waiting closets. By the end of the week, hair had been freshly washed, cut, plastered down, curled, or braided. By then every single person was in the grip of concert fever.

By ten o'clock on concert morning, people began to gather outside the school car. By noon there was a whole encampment chatting, joking, picnicking, and waiting for the performance to begin.

"Where do they all come from, Edith?" Mr. Merrill asked. "I can never figure it out."

After a few impatient guests climbed up the school room steps, Mr. Merrill stepped outside. "Please, everyone, the children want it to be a surprise."

"All right," someone called, "we'll wait. We don't mind. It's a holiday."

"Why should we mind?" came another voice. "Here are friends, here is good food."

There was a lot of laughter, then a glass of wine was held out by John Kusiak. "Mr. Merrill? Elderberry. It's good. Joe made it."

"It's delicious," Mr. Merrill said after he sipped the wine. "And I'd like to stay right here for a while, but..." He smiled and slipped back up the steps.

At ten minutes before two o'clock Mr. Merrill and his wife made a last survey of the school room. It had been transformed into a jungle, with lions, tigers, elephants, and monkeys peering through crepe-paper leaves.

"It's wonderful! Isn't it wonderful, Edith, what this group can do?" Mr. Merrill looked at his watch. "All right, everybody, take your places at the front. Eddie, you can open the door."

The crowd poured in: parents, babies, sisters, brothers, trappers, section hands, woodsmen, Eddie's whole family, all their relatives, and Eddie's dog. Eddie's brother stood and explained, "He doesn't like it outside because he's an inside dog."

When everyone was settled, Jenny, who was in charge, rose to welcome them and to announce the first item on the program. She looked at her notes. "I am very pleased..." She paused. With a rush, she started again. "What I mean is, I always love coming to Lost River. We all do. I'm so glad you're here." She cleared her throat. "And now..."

Teeny Crawford, pigtailed and ruffled, stood and recited "I Have a Little Shadow That Goes In and Out with Me" in a voice so small only a mouse could have heard it.

There was hearty applause, after which her father said, "I heard her, Ma, didn't you?"

Then the three Morin children got up to sing French-Canadian folk songs. Jenny was surprised but pleased when their father came forward to accompany them on his accordion. In no time everyone was clapping. Feet were tapped, tables thumped, babies jiggled, and the Morins had to sing two encores.

Before Jenny could announce the next number, Tony got up and walked straight to the centre of the room. From way at the back his father shouted, "Take your hands out of your pockets, boy!"

Tony glared but removed his hands and let them hang by his side. He gulped. The audience, plainly puzzled, waited.

"Mr. Merrill," he started, his voice coming out as a squawk. He cleared his throat and started again. "Mr. Merrill, I didn't think you could do it, but you done good. *Did* good. Believe me, Mr. Merrill, I've been to plenty of schools, so I should know. In my opinion," he finished with a burst, "this must be the best school in the whole world." To a roar of applause, stamping, and whistling, he sat down.

Jenny flushed pink with happiness. An earlier Tony, a defiant Tony, flashed through her mind. And now he had said, "the best school in the whole world." Oh, she was proud! Of course, it wasn't only her, she thought hastily.

When Jenny finally made herself heard, she announced

the next item on the program: a square dance called "Dip for the Oyster, Dive for the Pearl." Then she joined her schoolmates to form a square as the band started to play— Mr. Kusiak on fiddle, Mr. Morin on accordion, and Mr. Highwater on bass drum, which was really Mrs. Merrill's washtub turned upside down.

Right after the applause, Mr. Kusiak called for a second set. "Come on, folks. Four more couples up on the floor." So many joined in that they had two more sets whirling and dipping and diving.

Then someone sang out, "A Virginia reel!"

"A reel!" Jenny cried. "Everyone up in two long lines." The band struck up, and the dancers went forward and back, left and right, and then reeled down the line in pairs.

After that the party soared, and with it the babble and buzz of voices. When the talk died down, Jenny rose to give the final speech.

"I haven't written anything," she said. "It's so hard to find the words. And I'm not like Tony. I haven't been to lots of different schools, so I can't compare. But somehow I don't have to. I just know Tony's right— there's no other school in all the world like this one."

She sat down. This time the applause was so loud even the wailing babies couldn't be heard. When the cheers were over, Mrs. Merrill called out, "Good things to eat are on their way." Her helpers came through with such trays of sandwiches, cakes, and pies that soon every mouth was occupied.

Later, when the goodies were finished, the songs had been sung, and the talkers talked out, there was still spirit enough for cheer after cheer for the whole Merrill family.

"And don't forget the gerbils!" someone yelled.

"Well, Edith," Mr. Merrill said when everyone was gone, "another school year over. I'd say it was a good one, wouldn't you?"

"I'd say it was a great one," she answered.

Jenny, who had overheard, considered their words. A great year? Well, true, school was special. She had meant what she had said. But for her, it had been sort of mixed up. One thing was certain, though. Next year she wouldn't be taking charge at any concerts. She'd be much too busy playing violin solos.

That night in bed her thoughts turned to the next day. Tomorrow vacation would start. They'd get on the train and go to Glendale.

She could see Glendale, could smell it. Fields of daisies and buttercups and the sweet, sweet scent of clover. The farm horses ploughing the neighbour's field. Buck and Dandy. She could see the white star on Dandy's nose and feel the velvet of Buck's lips as he mouthed a piece of apple from her hand. And their family cottage. She saw it standing there, waiting for them, as always.

Then she remembered that it wouldn't be like always. Not this year. Not for her.

Cucumbers! She hoped her plan would work and that she'd like doing it.

Jenny tried to picture herself smiling and holding up a shiny jar of pickles. "Oh, yes, Mrs. Jones, I made them my— " But she soon fell asleep.

Seven

"Dad!" Brian shouted. "Here! These seats are the best."

"Why?" Mrs. Merrill asked.

" 'Cause they're near the observation platform."

Meg drew a deep breath. "Real trains smell different."

"Like better," Brian asked, "or like worse?"

"Like going far, far away."

"Oh, Glendale's not that far," Mr. Merrill said. "Maybe six hundred miles."

"But they're big miles," Meg insisted.

"Let's turn the seats to face each other," her mother suggested.

"So we can talk," Brian finished.

"There's only room for four, so I'll sit behind you," Jenny said. "I want to, anyway."

She moved to the window seat behind them, pleased to be by herself. Already they were buzzing away, and the train hadn't even started.

"Can I swim tomorrow? Did you bring my bathing suit?" Meg asked.

"Feels good, eh, Edith?" Mr. Merrill said.

"I'm hungry, Mom. Have we got any sandwiches?"

Jenny thought about the cucumber plants in the baggage room. She'd packed them in wooden boxes and had marked FRAGILE and PLANTS on all sides. Still, she thought, maybe she'd better go and make sure they were all right.

She strode through seven cars, enjoying the sense of freedom it gave her. In the baggage room the big doors to the platform were open, and the baggage men were still busy loading. One of the men looked up. "I know you. You're one of the Merrills. Saw your plant boxes coming in. See what we did? We put them together over there and then we walled them off with these cases. Safer that way. What are you planting?"

Jenny told him about the cucumbers.

"Timing's right," he said. "Good luck with them."

There was no hurry going back. She might as well enjoy being on a "real" train. As she strolled by the other passengers, Jenny wondered where they were going and why. Maybe the old man with the cello case on the seat beside him was a famous cellist. Maybe he was on his way to his last solo performance. The audience would clap and beg him for an encore...

As Jenny slid back into her seat, the conductor shouted "All Abooaard!" The train shuddered, jerked, and rolled on its way. Settling into her seat, she half heard the little tendrils of talk drifting back.

Mrs. Merrill sighed happily, "Oh, Matthew, isn't it grand?

Nothing to do but—"

"Mom, did you pack my running shoes?"

"When I get to the cottage—"

Dimly Jenny heard their voices. She closed her eyes, listening to the wheels pulsing *On the way, on the way, on the way*, and fell asleep.

$\mathcal{J}$/

"I always love this first day at the cottage," Mr. Merrill said, walking around the living room and swinging his arms back and forth. "I suppose I say that every year."

A chorus of "You sure do" and "Not again" greeted him.

"Well, it's just that I wish I didn't have to go off to that conference in a few days. You people are the lucky ones."

"I wish you didn't have to go, too," Mrs. Merrill murmured. She turned to the others. "Breakfast, everyone."

At the table they all talked at once.

"Can we go swimming right away?"

"Are the raspberries ripe yet?"

"Let's see if the Grover kids are here."

"Oh, Matthew, the space, the blessed space," Mrs. Merrill enthused. "I'm not going to do a single thing today. I'm just going to sit. You can all unpack and get the meals." She sighed with the very pleasure of the thought.

Meg looked anxious. "You wouldn't really not do anything, would you, Mom?"

Jenny didn't talk at all. She ate her breakfast at double speed.

"Are you in a race?" her father asked her.

"No, but I've got to get up to the farm and find Mr.

MacAllister. I have to get my cucumbers in. Maybe he'll help me take them over."

"Where's the farm, Jen?"

"It's really close. He sent me a map. You just go down the road, then you branch off to a little side road and you go all the way to the top of the hill. Well, bye. See you later."

She ran up the hill and arrived at the farm, breathless, to find Mr. MacAllister by the front gate, fixing a fence post. He didn't seem in any hurry. "Now, I imagine you must be Miss Jenny Merrill."

Still panting, she nodded.

"Lovely day, don't you think?"

She nodded again.

"How are your folks? Settling in nicely?"

She nodded for the third time.

Mr. MacAllister tested the fence post, then turned back to Jenny. "I hear they've been summering here from a long way back."

Jenny clenched her hands.

"Think I might have known a cousin of your father's—"

"Please, Mr. MacAllister, I hope I'm not hurrying you, but could you tell me about my cucumbers, what to do and everything?"

He leaned against the fence post and folded his arms. "Impatient young lady, aren't you?" But he smiled and added, "All right then, we can have a look. We go down here past the pumpkins and right over there by the fence. Nice sunny spot."

Jenny looked at her spot and then down over the rolling fields, green and gold in the sunshine. "Oh, it's beautiful here, Mr. MacAllister."

"Yes, it is. Now, did you do everything I told you?"

"Yes, exactly what you said."

"Plants came up nicely? All ready now?"

"Yes, they are. They're waiting at the cottage."

"I'll come by this afternoon with the wagon."

Jenny gave him her most beaming smile. "How can I ever, ever, thank you?"

"Wait a while. You haven't got any cucumbers yet."

She spent the next few days in a happy frenzy of digging, transplanting, and fertilizing.

Twice Brian came and helped her, although not for long. The first time he said he had to help his friend build a dog kennel.

"Oh, sure," Jenny said, "I don't mind." And she meant it.

The second time he said his friends were waiting for him. He added, "We're going to slide down the rocks under the falls."

"Oh, sure," Jenny said, "I don't mind." But she didn't quite mean it this time.

Meg came once with her gerbils. "To watch," she said.

At the end of the week Mr. MacAllister announced he needed her in the afternoons for the vegetable stand. On Monday he loaded the stand with fresh peas, early beans, lettuce, radishes, and boxes of ripe, red strawberries. He put a chair for Jenny in the cool of the big maple tree. "Just wait," he said. "It won't be long." Then he turned and went off.

He was right. The first two customers appeared almost right away. It was just like a play, she thought, when the curtain went up.

The ladies strolled up, baskets on their arms. They

examined the produce carefully. "Feel that, Millie," one said, squeezing a green bean. "Fresh as they come."

They also examined Jenny, although in a friendly way. "Now, you must be one of the Merrills," the one called Millie said. "Be sure to give our regards at home."

Finally they bought some beans and strawberries and strolled on.

Her first sale, Jenny thought, and it hadn't been hard at all. Others came in ones and twos, sometimes to look, maybe to buy, always to stop and chat.

Nobody was ever in a hurry here, Jenny thought. It was as if they were all on holiday.

One afternoon, as she was bringing out a fresh case of berries, a group of her friends dropped by. Somehow her elbow jarred one of the boxes, and the strawberries plopped and spattered the ground. Cheeks burning, she stooped to collect them.

The twins, Amy and Sue, chorused, "Oh, too bad!" The Fisher girls stepped daintily backward. Only Freddie bent down to help. "Nobody's fault," he muttered.

After a "How's it going?" Jenny's friends didn't have much to say. They bunched together with much giggling and jostling and hoisting of beach bags.

"We'd love to stay," one twin said.

"But we have to go," the other said.

"I really wish you could come," Freddie called as they backed off. And then they were gone.

Jenny's thoughts flamed. Why couldn't they have helped? Except for Freddie, they had just stood there and watched. She was angry, yet she longed to join them. Instead, she waved a very small wave at their departing backs.

The Glendale crowd, Jenny thought. Freddie was one of the nicest. The Fisher girls—they always had their noses in the air. But she'd always been closer to the twins.

Why was she doing this? she asked herself. Everybody was having fun but her. Even Brian and Meg had said they'd help, but had they?

That thought was chased by another. What was the matter with her? This was what she had wanted. Remember? Then some customers came by and there was no more time for brooding.

Mostly it was pleasant work at the stand, but by the end of the day Jenny was glad to go home to supper. Besides, mealtime was now the only occasion she saw her family.

But, she remarked to herself, all they wanted to talk about was picnics and the beach and cookouts. It was funny. She was there, but she wasn't. She was herself, but she felt like someone else.

At breakfast Brian's first words were: "Me and Ted are going fishing today. We're taking the rowboat. I'm making sandwiches, Mom."

"Yes? Well, good," Mrs. Merrill said. "And with the river only three feet deep you won't likely drown." She herself looked tanned and well.

Oh, the river! Jenny thought. With its sandy, pebbly beach and the little minnows nibbling at her feet. She longed for the feel of it.

"Jen, I bet you wish you could come," Brian said. "I do, too," he added hastily.

That did it. A fat tear slid down Jenny's nose and splashed onto the table.

"Well, now..." Mrs. Merrill looked up, surprised. She

waved the others away. "Jenny, dear, I thought this was the way you wanted things."

Jenny sniffed and kicked the table leg. "I do."

"Then what's the problem?" There was no reply, so Mrs. Merrill continued, "I guess it's not so easy when everyone else is having a good time."

Jenny nodded.

"But you chose to do this. So maybe it's time you stopped feeling sorry for yourself and just got on with the job."

Jenny looked at her mother with surprise. "I never heard you talk like that before."

"I never needed to."

Jenny was shaken by her mother's words, knowing they weren't lightly spoken. As she started for the farm, she felt both rebuked and relieved. And she was rather glad her father was in Toronto for a conference.

♪

By early August the cucumbers in Jenny's plot were green and glossy. Walking through the patch on a breezy, blue morning, she felt a surge of pride.

"It's the sun," Mr. MacAllister said, "and the good, warm days, though I must say, Jenny, you're a right good farmer. Well, we're getting toward the end now. Just pray we don't have an early frost."

But the next week the weather took a turn for the cooler. "Nothing to bother about," Mr. MacAllister said at first. But the temperature kept dropping, and he began shaking his head.

Fear chilled Jenny, too. What if there were a frost? What

if her crop were spoiled? What if it had all been for nothing? She found herself pacing the plot, eyeing the cucumbers, and feeling them, too. So far so good, but the temperature didn't climb and there were still ten days to go.

The fifteenth of August dawned dark and cold. For the first time Mr. MacAllister appeared worried. He glanced at the sky and frowned. "We could have a frost tonight."

For the first time Jenny felt a stab of concern—for him. It was his whole crop, she thought. The farm could even fail. "Mr. MacAllister, what should we do?"

"Have you got a thermometer at the cottage?"

"Yes, we do."

"If the temperature drops, you come back up here this afternoon."

"What about the stand?"

"Never mind the stand." He thought for a moment. "Have you got any old sheets?"

"I don't think so. But there are some burlap bags in the shed."

"Bring them."

"Can they really help?"

"Maybe."

The temperature went slowly down. At the cottage they knew what that could mean. Lunch was a quiet meal, and afterward Brian offered to help Jenny up the hill with the burlap bags.

"I'll be waiting here with cocoa and cookies," Mrs. Merrill said. "And I'll be hoping."

They plodded up the hill in the darkening afternoon.

"Brian," Jenny asked, "is that a snowflake?"

"I guess so. Only one, though."

Her heart sank.

When they got to the farm, the whole MacAllister family was out in the fields. Their two sons, Andrew and Pete, were setting out smudges, smoky fires, between the rows of pumpkins and squashes.

Mr. MacAllister was on his knees, covering the beans with canvas sheets. He creaked to his feet and rubbed his hands on his overalls.

"Evening, young Merrills. We've got the smudges started, but I don't think we'll get through the whole crop. Well, it helps, I suppose. Got the burlap? Good. Get to work and cover each mound. There's a knife over there. Split the bags if you need to. And mind the burlap doesn't touch the cucumbers. You might have to use sticks as props. I've got to get on with it now. Call if you need me."

Jenny and Brian thanked him and went to work in the fading light. They found it a finicky job, since the prickly plants didn't take to the burlap. So it was after dark when they finally got to their feet.

Brian rubbed his hands. "I can't even feel them. Come on, Jenny, let's go."

"You go."

"What do you mean? Why not you?"

"Well, the MacAllisters are still working over there. I'll stay and give them a hand."

Brian sighed. "All right. Come on, then."

It was close to midnight when they stumbled home, exhausted. Mrs. Merrill was waiting with cocoa and sandwiches. Jenny gulped the hot liquid, but she was too tired to eat. With a heartfelt "Thanks, Brian and Mom," she shuffled off to bed.

Although her body ached, she couldn't sleep. She imagined the plants lying limp and lifeless on the ground. Then she saw the violin receding in space until it was just a dot.

Jenny pushed back the covers, tiptoed into the big room, and lit one of the lamps. Then, after a hunt for pencil and paper, she sat at the table to write.

August 15, 1927

Dear Mr. Eaton,

I guess I might as well tell you now. You don't need to save my violin any longer, as it is no use.

We put burlap over the cucumbers tonight, but it is near freezing, so it is no good. I can't make the pickles, and I won't be able to pay for the violin. It is no use now, Mr. Eaton.

She signed her name, blew out the light, and went to bed.

Someone seemed to be shaking her.

"Wake up, Jenny!"

"Go away."

"Jenny, it's me, Brian. The crop is saved. Mr. MacAllister is right here. He's in the kitchen."

Jenny snatched up her robe and shot into the kitchen.

"Thought I'd come by," Mr. MacAllister said. "The crops made it through the night. Yours and mine. The temperature's back up. Guess we're safe for a while. Jenny, you take the day off. Bye now."

Jenny danced around the room and then plopped herself down at the table. It still had an ink stain from the night before. An ink stain? She flew back to her room, snatched the letter, and tore it into little pieces.

Meg, in the doorway, asked, "What are you doing?"

"Just tearing up something silly I wrote. Come on, Meg, I smell bacon."

At breakfast Jenny said between mouthfuls, "It feels like a holiday."

"Then let's celebrate," Brian suggested.

"Why not?" their mother agreed.

"A bonfire, okay, Mom?"

"Okay, Jenny."

"With hot dogs."

"We'll get them, Brian."

"And marshmallows."

"Those, too, Meggie."

Jenny sat there glowing. "We'll invite all our friends. Oh, and Freddie can bring his ukulele."

Brian thumped the table. "And you know what? The Grovers have some Roman candles left over from Victoria Day. Yahoo!"

Eight

For Jenny the celebration marked the end of the summer. True, there were ten days left of vacation. But with the cucumbers to harvest and the pickles to make, there wouldn't be much time for anything but work. Maybe hard work, she figured.

In fact, it was only two days after the bonfire that Mr. MacAllister said, "The cucumbers are ready, Jenny. Better pick them tomorrow. No good waiting."

This was the moment she had been dreading. Not so much the picking as the pickling, which was bound to follow. The truth was that she knew nothing at all about pickling, or how, or where she might do it.

She wound one leg around the other and bit her lip. "Honestly, Mr. MacAllister, I've been thinking and thinking, and I'm ashamed that I never—"

"Thought so," he said. "Use the summer kitchen. We do a lot of canning and pickling there. Got all the stuff. Ask my wife." Then he was off.

Jenny ran after him. "Just stop for one minute so I can thank you." But he didn't.

"No need," he said over his shoulder.

Harvest day dawned fair and cool.

"I'm coming to help you," Brian announced at breakfast. "And Jamie and Ted are coming to help me."

"You know, you've really got good friends," Jenny said. "Mine wouldn't come. I know they wouldn't. Maybe you're just nicer than I am."

"Naw," Brian said, "I told them this would be fun."

Jamie and Ted were ready and waiting when Brian and Jenny got to the farm. Ted rubbed his hands. "This is a first for me. Cucumbers, here I come."

"All right then," Jenny said, "let's get to work. The gloves are over there."

"Why gloves?" Jamie asked.

"Because Mrs. MacAllister said picking cucumbers is hard on the hands."

"Mine are tough," Ted boasted. "I don't need any gloves." But the spiny stalks were even tougher, and after a while he slipped on a pair.

They were all glad of the gloves, but not for long. "It's too slow this way," Jenny said, stripping hers off.

After that they picked barehanded. "Ouch," Jamie said. "Darn things are getting me." He wiped off a few drops of blood. "I thought this would be more like picking apples."

By noon they were hot and sweaty and the plot was less than half-picked. Around two o'clock Jamie stood and wiped his hands. "Listen, I'm real sorry. We didn't know it would take so long. We promised the others we'd meet them down at the beach."

Ted rose stiffly to his feet. "That's true. They'll be wondering what happened to us."

"Don't worry," Jenny said quickly. "Brian and I can finish."

They waved their friends on and bent back to work. Two hours later they straightened their sore backs and surveyed the cucumber crop, picked, basketed, and ready.

Jenny stretched. "You know something, Brian? I really respect farmers."

"Yeah, sure." He looked down toward the river. "I wonder if the guys are still at the beach."

Later, as Jenny bathed her bleeding hands, she told herself that tomorrow was bound to be easier. Pickling couldn't be as hard as picking. And she promised herself that when it was over, she would never, ever again make pickles.

$$\text{♪}$$

Word about the pickling had gotten around. All Glendale seemed to know about it, and everyone in the town had advice to offer.

"Plenty of dill."

"Easy on the dill."

"Now mustard seed, that's what counts."

"Well, there's some put garlic into everything."

"I guess they mean well," Jenny told her mother, "but they make my head spin."

"Then don't listen," her mother said. "You'll manage when the time comes."

That soothed Jenny, but only somewhat. She still had doubts and fears.

But it was her mother who had remembered that jars would be needed. She had quietly rounded up dozens of secondhand jars. "They cost less," she explained, "and they're just as good."

"Oh, Mom, I can't even pay you back for them."

"Plenty of time for that when the last pickle in the last jar has been sold to the last buyer."

They both laughed, and Jenny felt better.

On pickling day Meg volunteered to help.

"But what could you do, Meggie?" Jenny asked. "The trays of jars will be heavy to carry, and besides, you'll get tired in a few minutes and want to go home to your gerbils."

"No, I wouldn't. I'd stay all morning and I'd help."

So Meg came and measured the salt and sugar and the spices for the pickling brine. She went home before noon, quite pleased with herself.

"Couldn't have managed without you," said Mrs. MacAllister, who had been supervising every step.

Soon the back kitchen was hot and steamy. From time to time Jenny mopped her face with an old handkerchief, but by noon she had scrubbed and rinsed the cucumbers and steeped them in the spicy brine.

Mrs. MacAllister sniffed the big pickling kettle. "It's going to be a good batch," she said approvingly. "Now, we'll let them steep overnight, and tomorrow we'll finish the job."

The next morning Jenny set off early by herself. Brian had mumbled something about working on the dog kennel.

"Sure, sure, I don't mind. You've done enough," Jenny said. "And you'd better mean that," she said under her breath as she plodded up the hill.

When Jenny arrived, Mrs. MacAllister was already in the summer kitchen, assembling the kettles and pots. "Jenny, you'd better start on the jars."

"What should I do to them?"

"They have to be washed, rinsed, and sterilized. I'll finish the pickling mixes."

A wave of relief swept over Jenny. What would she have done if Mrs. MacAllister had said, "Oh, here you are, Jenny. Go ahead and make the pickles."

She busied herself with the jars until two heads appeared inside the kitchen door. Heads only, since the bodies remained carefully outside.

"Hi there, Amy. Hi, Sue," Jenny said to the heads.

The girls smiled. One said, "We just came to see how you were getting along."

"But we can't really stay," the other one added.

Mrs. MacAllister didn't seem to have heard them. "Aha! Here to help. Good. I knew your friends wouldn't let you down, Jenny."

She took a firm hold of two arms and drew the owners inside. "Now, Amy, you pack the cucumbers in the jars. Sue, you add the dill."

Amy opened her mouth to say something, but Mrs. MacAllister kept right on talking. "Now, we're really getting on. We'll soon have those jars cooling on the shelves. I don't know what we'd have done without you girls."

The girls seemed dazed but did as they were asked. Meanwhile Mrs. MacAllister, with one eye on the kettles and one eye on them, kept up a running conversation. But the minute she stopped for breath, a faint voice whispered, "We have to go now," and the two helpers vanished.

Mrs. MacAllister watched them leave and her lips tightened. "They've a busy schedule, I've no doubt."

About two hours later Mrs. MacAllister wiped her hands on her apron and said, "Well, Jenny, there we are. Now, when you label the jars, be sure you advance the date for use. The pickles need time to ripen." Together they surveyed the rows of jars.

"It looks like an army," Jenny said.

"It is. Your army, and you're the general. Tomorrow you move the troops."

"Mrs. MacAllister?"

"Yes?"

"Well, when I started with all this, I thought I could do everything myself. But I couldn't have done it without you."

"A little help, that's all."

"I don't know how to thank you, Mrs. MacAllister. I haven't even got anything to thank you with."

She patted Jenny's shoulder. "There's nothing to thank me for. I was glad to help."

The last few days at Glendale were a blur for Jenny, but some events did stand out. There was the big welcome for her father, back from the conference in Toronto. And then there was the lunchtime when Mr. MacAllister dropped by to ask if he could have fifty jars of pickles for the Glendale fall fair.

Fifty jars. Just like that! Jenny's spoon stopped halfway

to her mouth. She jumped up and threw her arms around his neck. "Could you? Oh, that would be wonderful."

Flustered but pleased, he said, "They'd sell fifty jars, easy. Now what about the price? We were thinking of twenty-five cents a jar."

"Twenty-five cents? That much?" She turned to the lunch table. "What do you think, everybody?" Except for Meg, they all agreed that twenty-five cents was a fair price. Meg said she didn't have twenty-five cents.

After that came the packing. Mrs. Merrill looked at the piles of luggage and sighed. "All these things you people had to take and half of them never used. Well, let's get on with it."

They did get on with it, but not very fast, because friends kept dropping by.

Jenny, of course, was busy with her jars. After removing the fifty for the Glendale fall fair, she carefully repacked the remaining one hundred and fifty. When that was done, she dusted off her hands and sat back. After a minute or two, she slipped outside into the late-August sunshine.

In a field across the road stood the ruins of a house and a once-lovely garden. Asters, chrysanthemums, and lilies still pushed their way through the undergrowth. She picked all the flowers she could carry and started up the road to the farm.

Mrs. MacAllister was out in front, sweeping off the doorstep. "Here." Jenny held out the flowers. "They're for you. It's nothing much, but we're leaving and...they're for you."

Mrs. MacAllister looked at the flowers and then at

Jenny. "Now, that's really kind."

"Oh, Mrs. MacAllister, you're the one who's really—Well, bye." Jenny blinked and hurried down the steps for the last time to her own patch of ground, empty now—no mounds, no vines, and no cucumbers.

Slowly she moved to the pasture where the cows placidly chewed their cud. It was as if this were an ordinary day, Jenny thought. As if she wasn't leaving. She patted the brown cow nearest the fence. "Try to remember me," she said, and started down the hill. Turning back for one last look, she walked slowly back down to the cottage.

Even before she opened the door she could hear her mother say, "Brian, did you bring the croquet things in? Matthew, have you found the key?" Then her mother turned to her. "Oh, Jenny, there you are. Bessie Miller was just in. Her sister's visiting from Longford, and when she heard about your pickles, she said she'd take twenty-five jars for their church bake sale. She said she'd be back. Look, there she is now."

And so the last thing Jenny did was to open one of the boxes, take out twenty-five jars, and pack it up again. And then, finally, they left for the train station.

Standing on the platform, they watched the engine pull in. It was like a beast, Jenny thought. A huge, black, steaming beast coming to carry them home. And suddenly summer was over.

On the train they stretched and spread and settled themselves. Brian yawned. "My friends think it's very funny that we have to take a train to get to our home, which is a train. Anyway, part of one."

Jenny looked up. "Maybe they're jealous."

She tried to settle down after the flurry of leaving, and to think of ways to sell her pickles. But her mind kept sliding off the subject, and in no time, she was asleep.

Nine

"Home," Meg said to the gerbils. "You're home." She turned to Brian. "They're so happy."

"How can you tell?"

"By their faces."

"It's too bad they can't read the sign on the side of the car. They'd like that."

The sign, made from cedar branches, read WELCOME HOME, MERRILLS in giant green letters.

"That just looks so special, Edith," Mr. Merrill said. "I'm going to get out my Brownie and take a few snapshots."

"As you often say, Matthew, it warms the heart."

"More than the heart," he replied as two women approached with covered pans. "I think it's going to warm the stomach."

They were only the first. Soon the school car was filled with friends, all wanting to welcome them back.

Eddie Kusiak nudged his way through the crowd. "Hey,

Brian, you like the sign? Me and Francine and Vic made it."

"It's super," Brian said.

One of the last to come was Mrs. Highwater. She greeted Mrs. Merrill and held out a basket made from sweetgrass and filled with herbs.

"It's beautiful," Mrs. Merrill said, fingering the woven pattern. "I knew the Cree people made these baskets. I've always wanted one."

"I made it to welcome you home," Mrs. Highwater said. Then she slipped down the stairs just as Mrs. Beeson puffed up with a chicken potpie.

"Came up on the morning train. Twenty-five minutes, that's all. Thought I'd save you cooking," she said, gulping for air. "I see other people had the same idea. Well, it can't hurt. I'm not staying, though. You people must be tired. But I'm looking forward to a good, long talk."

"It wouldn't be about cucumbers?" Jenny said, and the Merrills burst out laughing.

$\oint$ /

Three days before school began, Mr. Merrill was at his desk in the school room, surrounded by papers, textbooks, maps, and callers—some to talk about school and family matters, others there just to say hello. With vacation over it seemed as if almost everyone wanted to speak to him.

Jenny, too, was far from idle. Help was needed to get things ready for the school term. With Brian she cleaned the school room, set out the desks, checked the supply lists, and sharpened pencils. Her hands were constantly busy. So was her mind. All she could think about was pickles.

One hundred and twenty-five unsold jars seemed more like a thousand. How was she going to sell them? It wasn't like Glendale up here. There was no place large enough to have a fall fair or anything like that.

The violin seemed to shimmer in the middle distance. During the day, she was too busy, and at night she was too tired to listen for its music.

Two days before the start of school Jenny had just rechecked a shining school room when her sister came through with a heavy box. "Look, Jenny, I brought Mom's geraniums."

"Look out, Meg. Don't tilt them!" But it was too late. The floor was covered with earth, broken pots, and geraniums.

Meg bit her lip. "I didn't mean to."

"It's all right," Jenny said. "It's not your fault. Get the broom and the dustpan. We'll soon clean it up." Glumly she set to work, though she was fed up with cleaning.

"Hello, hello, hello!" a voice piped up. "Look what the wind blew in. Me, Tony—the big noise!"

Presto! For Jenny, the mess was a joke and the day was bright. "Oh, you, Tony," she said. "It's good to see you."

"What happened here?"

"Nothing. A little accident."

When Meg brought the broom in, he said, "Give it to me. I'm Tony, the cleanup man." And, a few pots later, flowers and order were restored.

Tony dusted off his hands. "So," he said to Jenny, "how was the summer? Swimming and tennis and stuff like that?"

They sat in the school room, and Jenny told him all about her summer. She ended with the hundred and twenty-five jars of pickles and her problem. How was she going to sell them?

He walked up and down the aisle, tapping the desks and talking, partly to himself, partly to Jenny. "Hmm, pickles. People like pickles. Why should they be so hard to sell? Twenty-five cents a jar. You're almost giving them away." He ran one hand through his hair. "Listen, Jenny, I've got an idea. At every stop you have at least one evening of bingo or something. So why not do it like this? Suppose Brian stands up and says, 'Now, everybody, keep quiet. Jenny has something to say.' Then you get up and tell them about your pickles. They're right there on the table, and there's such a rush you can hardly get near them." With a satisfied smile, he folded his arms.

Jenny was silent.

"What's the matter?" he said with a puzzled frown. "You don't like my idea?"

"Well, it isn't that. Not exactly. I mean, it might be a good idea, but I'm not sure my parents would like it."

When Jenny spoke of it at suppertime, she found her family hesitant.

Mr. Merrill said, "I know, Jenny, it does seem like a good idea, but people who can't afford it might buy them just to please. And yet it's not a bad idea. Trust Tony!"

Jenny smiled. "Listen, Dad, just this minute I had another idea. What if I put a notice on the blackboard saying 'Homemade pickles for sale. Twenty-five cents a jar. See Jenny in the kitchen'? Then people wouldn't feel obliged, would they? I mean, they'd only buy them if they really wanted to."

Mrs. Merrill looked up from her knitting. "That strikes

me as a good plan."

Mr. Merrill considered the proposal. "Yes," he said slowly, "I think that's a fair compromise. That way there's no pressure on anyone."

Jenny drew a deep breath. A small step forward. And tonight was her night in the special berth. It had turned out to be a lovely day, after all.

At breakfast the next morning Meg stared out the window. "The trees don't look real. If I had my paintbox, I'd paint them the reddest red in the world and the brightest yellow and the blackest green."

"That's exactly the colours they are," Brian said. "And they are real."

"Yes, but you know what she means," Jenny said. "It's so beautiful that you think it can't be true."

"And it's the last day before school," Brian mourned.

"Why don't we do something special?" Jenny suggested.

"That's an idea," Brian said.

"Mom, could you do without us for a while?" Jenny asked.

"I'll have to manage."

"What should we do, Brian?" Jenny questioned.

"I know! Why don't we go by the river to the place where it gets lost?"

"Where the blackberries grow?"

"Mom, if we pick berries will you make a pie?" Brian asked.

"I guess I could, but if you're going, get started soon. And be careful of the brambles."

They skipped off with a pail apiece. Crossing an open field, they jumped a tiny brook. All except Meg.

"Jump," Brian said.

"Too big."

"It is not. Jump."

She almost made it. Thoughtfully she examined her wet foot. "One foot jumps better than the other," she explained.

Brian was quite annoyed. "You don't have to be such a baby."

They passed a stand of golden birches and then went down through the dark green forest floor. Out in the open once again, they were close to the bank of the river. It burbled along and then, quite suddenly, disappeared into the ground. The three stood and watched, pails in hand.

"Who know, why it goes?" Jenny said. "That's poetry, in case you didn't know."

"Elves live there," Meg whispered. "And they can't come out because the river won't let them."

"Oh, I think the river would let them," Jenny said. "They just don't want to come out."

Brian shook his pail. "Did we come here to talk about elves or pick blackberries?"

He started up a little hill and the others followed. There, the berries hung heavily on the close-packed bushes. Now the pails came into action. Except for an "ouch" or two, all talking stopped while they picked.

Meg moved away a little to some smaller bushes. The others also moved about in search of the choicest berries.

As she picked, Meg hummed to herself. She couldn't see the others, but she could hear them moving. One of them was coming very close. She knew who that would be. "Brian!" she shouted. "This is my bush. Go away!" She stared through the parted bush, but the face staring back was black and hairy.

"Ahhhhh!" she yelled, and the bear took to its feet and disappeared down the hill. Brian and Jenny rushed to Meg just as she burst into tears. "He made me spill my berries," she sobbed.

They offered her some of their berries, but she insisted they help pick up her own spilled ones. After that they hurried back to the train car.

When the tale was told at home, Meg was given a hero's welcome. As for the blackberry pie, it was deep and delicious. It would have been even deeper, Meg said, if a thief hadn't come her way.

The first day of school began with a salvo of barking. A large malamute kept giving voice—endlessly, it seemed. "What is it with him?" Mr. Merrill muttered. "Duty or pleasure?" He went outside to investigate. The dog moved off to a grove of cedars, and Mr. Merrill followed.

There, sheltered by the trees, stood two small children. Their father, nearby, came slowly forward. Mr. Merrill greeted him warmly. "Are these two new pupils?" he asked.

"I would like them to go to school," the father said. "And they would like to go to school, even though they're very shy."

"Is there a problem then?"

"We've been told the school is only for the railway families. I'm a trapper."

"Pure nonsense," Mr. Merrill said. "The school is for everybody."

"Then I'll build a shelter near the tracks and we'll live there while the school car is in Lost River."

After that Mr. Merrill asked both pupils and bystanders to come to the end of the car so they could join in the raising of the Union Jack.

As they were filing into school, Jenny thought to herself that it was almost like a party when they raised the flag. The grown-ups seemed sorry when their children went inside, because they couldn't come.

Just before school ended that day, Mr. Merrill announced there would be bingo on Tuesday night and everyone in Lost River was invited.

On these get-together nights the blackboard was always cleaned and ready for special announcements. That Tuesday Jenny's pickle notice was first on the list. She watched and waited. Probably no one would ask her, she told herself. She shouldn't expect it.

But a few people did. Janie Wilson's mother went straight to the kitchen and put down her fifty cents. "Two jars, please," she said. And added, "I wouldn't miss this."

An elderly trapper found his way to the kitchen. "Pickles! It's so long since I've tasted one that I hardly remember what they're like."

"I hope these will refresh your memory pleasantly," Jenny said.

"You're a well-spoken young lady," he replied, bowing. "I'll certainly let you know."

He was a trapper, Jenny mused, but he talked like someone out of a book. She really liked him.

After that Tony appeared in the kitchen, money in his hand. "You the pickle lady?"

"Oh, come on, Tony, I know you're walking back to Lake Lucy tonight. You can't take a pickle jar with you."

"Wrong. Not walking. Staying over with the Highwaters. It's, like, a present for them."

"Have they ever tasted pickles?"

"I dunno, but they will now."

During that fall, Jenny sold three or four jars at every settlement. It was slow going, but her hopes were on the rise.

It came to her quite suddenly as she washed the supper dishes that she should write to Mr. Eaton again. Thank goodness she had torn up that letter at the cottage. Now she could write and tell him she was really on her way. And to be sure this time to keep a violin for her. He would want to know. She smiled and swirled the dishwater around.

"Hey, Jenny," said Brian, who was passing by. "Get on with those dishes."

"Oh, you don't like the way I do them? *You* do them."

"I love the way you do them," he said, moving fast.

Later Jenny sat down with pen and paper.

October 14, 1927

Dear Mr. Eaton,

I guess you're surprised I haven't written in such a long time. It was because I was very busy growing cucumbers—that's the only reason.

Now the pickles are made and I am selling them. Half

my jars are sold. I know I still have a long way to go, but I really think I can do it.

So, what I am saying is, please keep my violin for me. Please don't think I have forgotten it, or anything like that.

I will write to you again soon. I hope that you and your family are very well.

Sincerely yours,
Jenny Merrill

She folded the letter, then sealed and stamped it. Mr. Gauthier, who was playing chess with her father, looked up from the game. "Got a letter to mail, Jenny? Give it to me. I'm going south on the 9:27. It'll get there faster."

In the middle of the night Jenny sat bolt upright in bed. What had she said in her letter? *Half the jars are sold.* If half the jars were sold, she had twenty-five dollars! Enough to pay for her violin now!

She leaped out of bed, streaked into the school room, danced, and sang a soundless song.

Back in bed she thought, Oh-oh. She had been really stupid. She could have ordered her violin right then and there, and she could have paid for it.

Never mind. She would write tomorrow and explain everything. And this time she'd send the money and say please send her—oh, how could she wait!

In the morning, as soon as it was light, she wrote the second letter. She dated it October 15 and circled the date in red.

It was all a big mistake because I have $25.00 right now. I'll even have money left over. It all happened because I forgot to do my accounts. But everything is wonderful now.

Of course, I will keep on selling the pickles to pay for my lessons, but I am sending the violin money with this letter. Could you please send me my violin right away?

I might not be writing to you a lot after I get my violin, but I will certainly let you know how my lessons are going, when I find a teacher.

Thank you for everything you have done for me.

Sincerely,
Jenny Merrill

Jenny floated through the next few days. She wondered what Mr. Eaton would say when he got her second letter. She wondered if he would be surprised that she had earned the money. Maybe he would just think, *Well, I knew she could do it.* Maybe he would miss her writing to him. Of course, when she gave a concert, he could come to hear her.

She saw herself in a great concert hall, coming onstage for the tenth curtain call, bowing graciously as the audience clapped and clapped. Sometimes she imagined she was right here in the school car, magically enlarged to hold every single person from every single place along the line. She would stand in the kitchen in a filmy blue dress, waiting, violin in hand, as her father—no, as Mr. Eaton, the special guest, introduced her to the audience.

"And now, I would like to present Miss Jenny Merrill, the brilliant young musician who has honoured us by choosing the finest violin the T. Eaton Company has to offer."

Then she would walk through to the school room, ignoring Tony, who was trying to catch her eye, and she would play like an angel. She leaned on the school room broom—she and Brian were supposed to be cleaning up—to consider whether her playing might yet be angelic.

"Hey, Jenny," Brian said, nudging her, "the mail's in. Meg says there's a letter for you."

She dropped the broom and ran straight into Meg with the letter. "Oh, sorry, Meg. My letter? Thanks."

Anxious fingers ripped the envelope. It was too soon to be a reply to her second letter, the one with the money. She hoped it wasn't a reply to the first. It was.

October 17, 1927

Dear Jenny Merrill,

This letter is in reply to yours of October 14 concerning the reservation of the Superior Model Violin priced at $18.50, as specified in the 1927 spring catalogue.

In your letter you stated you did not at present have sufficient funds for purchase but believed this might be a possibility in the near future. The purpose of this letter is to advise you that you need no longer save toward the acquisition of the model you have selected since, regrettably, it is no longer available.

Is it not possible, however, that another model might do? Our second violin, while not equivalent, is also a fine instrument. We would gladly put one aside for you.

Please write at your earliest convenience, advising us of your intentions. Once again, our regrets,

D. B. Mann
Order Department
T. Eaton Co.

Jenny dropped the letter on a desk and lowered herself into the seat. She sat there, unmoving, in the fading light. In their own quarters lamps were lit, and in the kitchen pots clattered, dishes clinked, and the scent of a simmering stew stole its way right through the car. But not to Jenny.

When Meg came to call her to supper, she followed, unprotesting, and sat at her place, but neither spoke nor ate.

In the comforting glow of the oil lamps the others ate, made small talk, and waited for Jenny to speak. After a while she pushed back her chair and sighed a long sigh. "There's nothing that can be done now."

"Nobody can do anything unless you tell us what happened," Brian said.

In reply, Jenny handed him the letter. "You can read it aloud. Might as well."

When Brian finished, Mr. Merrill asked, "Should we talk about it, or would you rather not?"

"You can," Jenny said. "I don't mind. But there's nothing to say."

"That means you wouldn't accept the other model?"

"I don't want it, Dad. Don't you understand? I only want the one I want."

"But, Jen," Brian said, looking puzzled, "are you never going to play the violin because of this?"

For the first time Jenny wavered. "I suppose I could get another one from somewhere. I guess it's not the end of the world. But it wouldn't be the same! All the time I was cucumbering I was thinking of my violin in the catalogue."

There was an uneasy silence. Nobody could think of anything to say. From somewhere in the darkness came the long, drawn-out howl of a wolf.

Jenny smiled faintly. "I guess he knows how I feel." And on that note the Merrills turned down the lamps and went to bed.

Ten

At breakfast Jenny played with her food.

"Are you alive?" Brian asked.

"Of course I'm alive," she snapped, and stomped off into the school room just as the door shot open and Tony burst in, beaming like the sun.

"I've got great news. You're gonna be so happy. Listen to this! I found you a violin teacher. This man, he used to be a great violinist, and now he's old and wants to be with his son up the line. Are you lucky! He's a great teacher. My father said so." Tony paused for breath. "I already told him about you, and he's willing to teach you. Can you believe it?" He stopped short. "What's the matter, Jenny? You made of stone or something?"

Jenny told him what had happened.

He raised his arms and let them drop. "Listen—" he started, but the school bell rang and the others came crowding in.

The days dragged on. Everyone had heard about the great violin letdown, and everyone was very kind. But in private some people wondered why Jenny wouldn't accept the lesser model. "How different can it be?" they wondered.

Tony seemed baffled. When he came face-to-face with Jenny, he'd shrug, shake his head, and move on.

As for her family, they held little private conferences, but they all came to nothing.

The pickles continued to sell at the rate of four or five jars a week. But for Jenny there was no pleasure in it.

Still, she thought, she might as well sell them. She didn't want them. Dully she thought of the twenty-five dollars. Her violin money. What would she do with it now? She didn't know. She didn't much care.

By now it was late October. The trees were bare, the wind blew cold, and the ground was frozen. It looked the way she felt, Jenny thought. Nevertheless, when the whole school turned out to slide on the newly frozen pond, she slid with them. And when Vic's rear end cracked the ice, Jenny laughed with them.

Other pleasant things happened. Francine's cat had striped kittens. "All tigery," Meg said. And Jenny's team won a spelling bee.

Sometimes she forgot about the violin for whole minutes and even half hours. Once or twice it occurred to her that she was still quite young and that all kinds of things might yet happen—nice things. But overall a kind of dull ache remained.

For the Merrills the weeks were divided by the train car moving on. Once every week the engine came, snorting down the line and hauled them to their next stop: Blueberry Hill, Little Moose Lake, Greenwood, Lost River.

It was on a November afternoon at Lost River that it began to snow. At first a sprinkle, then a flurry, then a sky full of heavy white flakes.

In the school room all eyes were glued to the windows. "Now, look here," Mr. Merrill told the school. "It's exciting, I know, but you people have seen snow before. Is it possible to look at the blackboard instead of out the windows?"

It didn't seem to be, and finally he agreed to let his pupils out ten minutes early so they could have the first snowball fight of the season. They poured out into the new white world and exploded into action. Snowballs were hurled, tossed, flung, smacked, and smashed.

Jenny got one on the head, which trickled icily down her neck. She was just closing in on Vic, her foe, when her mother waved from the doorway. "Later," Jenny shouted, "I've got to get him!" Then she slammed Vic right in the face.

The afternoon darkened and the contestants drifted off. Brian lobbed one last shot at somebody's back. And then there was no one else left. In the dark blue silence he could hear the groaning and the cracking of the ice. From inside, the first lamp spilled out its warmth and light. He brushed the snow from his jacket and stamped his way up the steps.

Jenny, already inside, was helping Meg take off her things. A delicious smell wafted past all three noses.

"Pie," Brian said.

"Apple pie," Jenny added.

"With cinnamon and raisins," Meg said.

When they came into the kitchen, Mrs. Merrill looked up from the stove. "Oh, Jenny, there's a letter for you. It's on the table."

"I don't think I want a letter. They only bring you bad news. Brian, want a letter?" She held it up and jiggled it.

"Open it, silly," he said.

She examined the envelope. "It's from Eaton's. Honestly, I don't know if I want to open it."

"Fine, dear," her mother said, "but then you'll never know what was in it."

"Well, I guess that's true."

"Go on, Jen," Brian urged. "It won't bite."

"I wouldn't be so sure," Jenny said. But she slit the envelope and slowly unfolded the letter.

November 27, 1927

Dear Jenny Merrill,

I have been much disturbed since my last communication to you. It is most unusual that the T. Eaton Co. should fail in the delivery of merchandise advertised in the catalogue. I refer, of course, to the violin in question.

My assistants have scoured our shelves and our storage departments for the model requested, but to no avail. I, myself, placed a call to the Montreal branch on the chance of finding one there. With little hope I wired the

Winnipeg branch to find that, as expected, your model was no longer available.

Imagine, then, my surprise when a late call from Winnipeg informed me they had located one, and one only, tucked away on a bottom shelf. (Not the best of organization but, dear me, how fortunate.)

I ordered it shipped to Toronto at once so that I could ensure it was in perfect condition. And further—since I, myself, am not musical—I requested a professional musician to try it out in order to validate its quality.

He pronounced it to be in perfect condition and, he added, it was a remarkably fine instrument. I am therefore pleased to announce that the violin is, at last, on its way to you.

It remains only to wish you success and happiness in your chosen pursuit. Indeed, I am bound to say, you deserve it.

With all good wishes, I am, yours sincerely,

D. B. Mann, Manager
Order Department
T. Eaton Co.

Jenny was struck dumb. She sat, letter in hand, staring at nothing.

Brian waved his hands in front of her face. "Jenny! What is it?"

She held out the letter. "You can read it to the others."

The family gathered around, tense with concern. But by the time Brian had finished reading the letter, anxious faces had dissolved into smiles of relief, and a babble of voices filled the room.

Brian flung up his arms. "At last, at last."

"What a great turnabout," Mr. Merrill said.

"Now you can play for the gerbils," Meg added.

"I'm so glad it's ending this way," Mrs. Merrill finally said.

Jenny smiled a lot but said nothing. She had no words and only one thought: *This can't be happening. I must be dreaming.*

Only slowly did the numbness wear off. And as it did, a rising tide of pleasure grew within her. It wasn't the wild excitement that she had felt at first, but a quieter kind of happiness.

It was several days later that Jenny had an idea. It came to her while she was sharpening pencils in the schoo room. She walked straight up the aisle to her father's desk. "Dad," she whispered, "I've got to ask you something."

"Is it urgent?"

"Yes," she said, her face alight. "Let's have a celebration."

"Yes, well, fine, but this is school time. We'll talk about it later."

At the supper table Jenny reminded her father. "It's later now, Dad. Can we talk?"

"It's about a celebration," he told the others. "Jenny would like a flourish of trumpets."

"No, I wouldn't," she said. "I'd just like a get-together with everybody, but no bingo, no games, no movies."

"Is it to celebrate your violin?" Brian asked.

"I guess it is, but I don't want to tell everyone."

"Now let me get this straight." Her father tapped the table with the pickle fork. "It's to celebrate getting the violin, but you don't want to mention it."

"That's right."

"But, Jenny, you haven't even got the violin yet," Meg said.

"I know, but it doesn't matter. This time it's really coming."

"Why don't you want to tell people about it?" Mrs. Merrill asked.

"I don't know, Mom. It's just the way I feel. Anyway, why do we need an excuse for a party?"

"Well, that's true enough," her father said. "The school car's being here is excuse enough."

"Are we going to do anything special at the party?" Meg asked.

"I don't know, Meggie. Let's just invite the whole world and celebrate."

The first to arrive were a group from Greenwood. They had come up by train. "A party," Mrs. Beeson said. "I'd like to see sixteen miles keep me away." She arrived with her husband, the Wilsons, and two guests from Sudbury.

"Jim and Franco are coming up, too," she said. "I

wouldn't be surprised if they're a bit late. No train for them. They're breaking in a new dog team. I said, 'Jim, is there enough snow for the sled to run?' He said, 'Yes, oh, yes.' But the last I saw, the dogs were riding and the boys were pulling. Oh, well, it won't hurt them. It's only sixteen miles."

Mrs. Kusiak came up to the kitchen with a basket of little meat dumplings. "Pirogis," she said. "From my country. Very good. Here, Brian, try one."

He ate one and smacked his lips. "Want me to try another?"

She laughed. "Go to the party room. I'll help your mother."

The school room was filling up. Jim and Franco had finally arrived, looking tired and hungry.

"Just wait," Brian told them. "I'll get you something good from the kitchen."

The boys were followed by the three Morins and their father, with his accordion. Close on his heels came Tony, with a big hello for everybody.

Vic Eckonen came into the kitchen. "My mother's here," he said to Mrs. Merrill, beaming. "Her first time to a party. She said she learned English so well from you that now she can come, easy. But she sings really well in Finnish. She's been practising."

Mrs. Merrill looked through from the kitchen. Jenny had been right. They didn't need a reason for celebrating. Not here. And yet, why didn't Jenny want to tell everyone about the violin?

The sound of singing drifted into the kitchen and Mrs. Merrill's thoughts. "That must be Vic's mother," she said. "She has a lovely voice. Come on, Jean," she urged Mrs.

Beeson, "let's leave this stuff and go through."

When the applause died down, Mr. Morin started right in with his accordion. He played old songs, and everyone sang along.

After that Eddie Kusiak's father, Big John, was dragged forward by his wife to play his mandolin. "Not for him," she explained. "For us."

"Come, everybody, I will teach you a new dance. Easy step, the grapevine step. Everyone join hands. We step side and forward, side and back. We stamp and turn, step side and..." At first only the brave moved forward, but soon the floor was filled with swirling circles.

I love this, Jenny thought as she circled and stamped and twirled. *I love everything.*

There was a lull while the dancers collapsed, breathless, but pleased with themselves.

Instantly Tony was on his feet. "Listen, everybody, I've got something to say to all of you. In case you didn't know, soon we're going to have a great violinist. Already she has a teacher. Tomorrow comes the violin. Who is she?"

"Jenny!" roared the crowd, and they got to their feet and cheered.

A wave of feeling swept over Jenny. *They really care about me*, she thought.

When the cheers subsided, Mrs. Beeson stood up. "Now, I think," she boomed, "everyone should know that Jenny raised the money with her pickles, and she did it all herself."

"No," Jenny whispered. "No, please, Mrs. Beeson, stop."

Nodding and smiling, Mrs. Beeson lowered herself into her seat. Without any break Jenny found herself on her feet. The crowd waited.

"I want to thank you, Tony, Mrs. Beeson, everybody. You make me feel wonderful. But there's one thing I want you to know. I didn't do it all myself. I thought I could, but I couldn't. People helped me all along the way—starting with Mrs. Beeson."

There was a murmur of laughter and a protesting "I hardly did a thing" from Mrs. Beeson.

"And Mrs. Wilson for her words that started me off: 'Pickles. They're easy enough to make.'" The laughter swelled.

"And I haven't even said anything about my family, my special family, and the MacAllisters down in Glendale, and all the people who bought the pickles, and all of you, because—" her voice trembled "—without you I couldn't... I never could have done it."

There was a thunder of applause. When it was finished, Mr. Morin held up his accordion. "Monsieur Merrill? Encore?"

Everybody except the sleeping babies joined in the encore.

When everyone had gone, the school desks had been pushed back in place, and the last dish had been washed and dried, Jenny put on her jacket. "Mom," she whispered, "I'm just stepping outside for some fresh air."

"All right, but don't stay long. It's close on midnight."

"I know. I'll keep right beside the rail car." Jenny tiptoed down the steps into the blackness. The spangled sky stretched overhead. She walked slowly, one hand touching the side of the car.

After a while she moved away a little and looked back at the school car. First the school-room lamp was snuffed and then the others until only one light was left. Still Jenny lingered. Soon, the violin, soon, the lessons. She smiled at the thought.

Then, in the darkness, she moved to her other world. Floating onstage, she tucked the violin under her chin and drew the bow across the strings...

MORE YA FICTION FROM BEACH HOLME

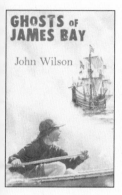

Ghosts of James Bay
by John Wilson
YA 9-13 $9.95 CDN $6.95 US ISBN: 0-88878-426-0

Fourteen-year-old Al is spending the summer on the shores of Ontario's James Bay with his eccentric archaeologist father, who is determined to find proof of the first explorers to visit the area. On their last day there, Al paddles his canoe away from the rocky, tree-lined shore and is strangely overtaken by a thick fog that disorients him. As the mist rolls over him, Al is startled to see a ship in the distance that he recognizes as the *Discovery*, whose captain was the ill-fated Henry Hudson. Is it a ghostly apparition?

Viking Quest
by Tom Henighan
YA 9-13 $8.95 CDN $5.95 US ISBN: 0-88878-421-X

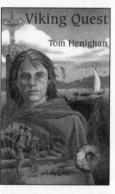

Fifteen-year-old Rigg, son of Leif Eriksson, loves mystery and adventure. In the early eleventh century, the boy finds both of these in abundance when his father sails away and leaves him behind in Vinland, the Vikings' precarious foothold on the wild Newfoundland coast. Soon, Rigg makes an amazing discovery. The Vikings aren't alone in this alien land. But who inhabits it with them? Demons, giants, ghouls, or another human tribe, one that equals the Norse invaders in skill and bravery?

Tiger in Trouble
by Eric Walters
YA 9-13 $8.95 CDN $5.95 US ISBN: 0-88878-420-1

In this sequel to Eric Walters's bestselling *Tiger by the Tail*, Sarah and Nicholas Fraser set off to spend a week at zoo camp, compliments of their absent father. When Sarah overhears a conversation late one night and learns of the sinister plans for Kushna the tiger, she and Nicholas once again must spring into action to save an endangered animal. They need help to do it, and that means turning to the only person they know who can—Mr. McCurdy!

BEACH HOLME PUBLISHING ◆ WWW.BEACHHOLME.BC.CA

MEMBER OF SCABRINI MEDIA

Quebec, Canada
2001